SUNDAY DAFFODIL AND OTHER HAPPY ENDINGS

This is P. Robert Smith's second novel.

P. ROBERT SMITH

Sunday Daffodil and Other Happy Endings

VINTAGE BOOKS
London

Published by Vintage 2010

2 4 6 8 10 9 7 5 3 1

Copyright © P. Robert Smith 2010

First published in Great Britain in 2010 by Vintage
Vintage
Random House, 20 Vauxhall Bridge Road,
London SW1V 2SA

www.vintage-books.co.uk

Addresses for companies within The Random House Group
Limited can be found at: www.randomhouse.co.uk/offices.htm

The Random House Group Limited Reg. No. 954009

A CIP catalogue record for this book
is available from the British Library

ISBN 9780099535232

The Random House Group Limited supports The Forest Stewardship
Council (FSC), the leading international forest certification
organisation. All our titles that are printed on Greenpeace approved
FSC certified paper carry the FSC logo. Our paper procurement
policy can be found at www.rbooks.co.uk/environment

Typeset by Palimpsest Book Production Ltd,
Grangemouth, Stirlingshire

Printed and bound in Great Britain by
CPI Bookmarque, Croydon CR0 4TD

For Victor, love Dobe

1

It was always going to have a happy ending. My life, I mean. But I guess most people must think that, otherwise everybody'd be going about with their face in a goddam fit, thinking about how maybe they were going to end up in some crummy hospital dying with some crummy disease to the sound of crummy cockroaches scuttling round the floor all night, which could really skew a person's outlook on life. I guess people like a happy ending. I guess it's only human nature, and you can't blame them for that. Of course, whether they get one or not is another matter entirely.

Don't get me wrong, though. I don't want to give you the wrong impression or anything. If there's one thing I hate it's a cynic. I really do. I can't stand that. If I ever meet someone who's always pointing out the bad side of things, you know, just because they think it's kind of impressive to have this black outlook on life, I'm always the first to say, 'Man, you're nothing but a big fat phoney.' Actually, I might not say it, but I'm certainly the first to think it. And if they turned around and actually said, 'Hey, Montanna, what do *you* think?' I'd probably say something really positive, just for the hell of it, even if I was feeling personally really low.

Another thing I'm not too crazy about, apart from cynics, is when you go to read something, a book or even just some article in a magazine, and you have to wade through so much detail just to get to the point, you finally can't even be bothered, and just give the hell up. As far as I'm concerned, if you're going to tell a story, or even just a joke, too much detail can be a real killer. It really can. Personally, I stop paying attention after about twelve seconds if whatever it is hasn't got to the point. If it hasn't got to it by then, I can't even be bothered. Which is why, instead of boring you with a whole bunch of stuff that isn't even important anyway, like what colour my eyes are (green), or whether or not I have a sweet tooth (I do), I'm just going to jump right in at the deep end, so to speak, with me stepping off the kerb into the path of that goddam speeding car.

BAM!

Now, that's definitely something I wouldn't recommend to anyone but the most dedicated thrill-seeker. By all means jump off tall buildings, skateboard down mountainsides, even experiment with a little fashionable self-amputation, but avoid getting hit by a speeding automobile if you can possibly help it.

I was on my way home from Moriarty's, which is a place Louie Louie and me while away our precious youth. As a matter of fact, I spend just about half my life there, if you want to know the truth. I'm like part of the furniture or something. We both are. Of course, you haven't met Louie Louie yet, but don't worry, you will. He'll be easy to recognise, too. He'll be the sonuvabitch eating my breakfast.

Louie Louie's actually my best friend, although you wouldn't think it judging by the way I talk about him. I say all kinds of stuff about him, most of it pretty insulting, to say the least. Actually, if you were to overhear me talking about him, you'd probably think he was my biggest enemy or something. I've never got a good word to say about him, but it's nothing compared to what he says about me. We've known each other for ever, and take it from me, he's a real genuine pain in the side. He really is. Always has been.

I wasn't going to, but I might as well tell you about when we first met. It was our first day at school, and he just came straight up to me in the playground and punched me right on the nose.

Pow!

Just like that.

Of course, I socked him straight back, and pretty soon the whole school was cheering us on.

'*Fight! Fight! Fight! Fight!*'

Kids just love a fight. It really brings out something special in them, even really quiet, shy kids. E*specially* really quiet, shy kids. Maybe it's the anonymity of the crowd. They can be part of the bigger picture without actually having to stick their own neck out. Really quiet, shy kids are probably just the kind of kids who grow up to join mobs. You see it all the time in the movies. If there's ever any lynching to be done, for example, it's always the quiet, shy, respectable citizens who are all for it. 'Lynch the sonuvabitch!' they're always hollering. 'String him up!' Of course, they're as contrite as hell afterwards, but it really gets their blood up at the time. I guess it breaks the monotony of being such decent citizens the rest of the working week. And there's another thing about fights, too. No one ever gives a fig what it's about, but they always take sides.

'I'm going for *that* guy.'

'No way, that guy *stinks*. I'm going for the other guy.'

Miss Cuthbert, fresh off the education production line, and all shiny and new, like plastic, finally broke it up, much to everyone's disappointment, except maybe Louie Louie's and mine. We'd been slogging it out for what seemed like about two hours, but was probably more like a minute at the most, and to be honest, really weren't getting anywhere. So being sent to our corners by the teacher, which is pretty much universally regarded as an honourable draw, no matter who's getting the worst of it, particularly when you're five and it's your first day at school, wasn't such a bad result. She even made us make nice and shake hands, and even though Louie Louie pulled a face at me that was almost as ugly as his regular one, we've been best friends ever since.

Curiously enough, it was also the occasion of my first falling in love. Love at first sight, no less, just like in the movies.

I went on to cherish this secret love – for shiny, new, plastic Miss Cuthbert, naturally – for a full six months. Right up to the time, in fact, of her sudden and mysterious disappearance mid-year, mid-week, mid-morning coffee break, which, incidentally, has never been satisfactorily explained. Local legend has it she left a half-drunk cup of coffee and an iced donut sitting on her desk.

A single delicate bite had been taken out of the donut.

But as I was saying, I was on my way home from Moriarty's. I was nearly there, too. Only a couple of blocks away. I've actually heard this is the most common place for road accidents, I guess because people start thinking about what they're going to do once they get there, like how good it'll feel to kick off their shoes, or to knock back a couple of frozen daiquiris or whatever, instead of concentrating on driving or not stepping in front of speeding cars. I remember I was humming an old show tune, an Irving Berlin ballad. 'I've Got My Love to Keep Me Warm.' I know most people my age haven't even heard of Irving Berlin, or Cole Porter, or the Gershwins, but I just love that stuff. I think it's just as elegant as hell. In fact, I used to nearly drive my parents crazy playing it all the time. I'd play it Night and Day. Day and Night. I couldn't get enough of it. It used to goddam kill me, it was so elegant. I'd imagine I was living it up at the Ritz, or someplace, or the Waldorf. Living on champagne and credit. I even used to listen to it on this terrifically old gramophone player that my parents had as an *orn*ament. They'd never *played* it in their lives. They didn't even have anything to play *on* it. Then what happened was, because I was playing them all the time, or maybe because they wanted their precious ornament back, one day they tossed my entire collection of old seventy-eights in the trash. Just like that. And I hadn't just found them up in some crummy old attic, either. I'd coll*ect*ed them. I must have swallowed half a pound of dust trawling through some of the crummiest

5

junk shops you've ever seen just to find them. People thought I'd developed a smoker's cough, but what I'd developed was a *dust* cough. So as you can imagine, I was pretty sore about them just tossing them in the trash like that. In fact, I was so sore I didn't speak to them for a month. But guess what? They didn't even notice.

And now there I was, only a couple of blocks away from hearth and home, having just stepped off the kerb in front of that lousy speeding car, sprawled in the middle of the road like a centrefold or something, *pan*caked. And the funny thing was, I still couldn't get that crackly old show tune out of my head.

There wasn't any pain. If there had been, I guess I'd have been screaming my head off. I have a very low pain threshold, apparently. I've been tested for it and everything. I'll scream my head off at just about anything, if there's pain involved. In fact, when I was a little kid and I had to go to the dentist I'd scream so much we had to keep changing dentists. We didn't want to, they insisted. I guess the last thing you want, when you're a dentist, is a waiting room full of already nervous patients and some kid inside screaming his lungs out every time you so much as stick a needle in his soft, tender gums or try and rip a tooth out. No one wants to hear that. But then, because there wasn't any pain, I began to think I must have been paralysed or something, which made me extremely nervous. The reason it made me extremely nervous – or at least *one* of the reasons – was that the thought of a lifetime of being given sponge baths flashed into my mind all of a sudden, and in particular how embarrassing it would be, and whether it would be worse being given them by some frumpy, middle-aged, matronly type, or by someone young and attractive, possibly with a corny French accent. But then I felt the hot asphalt burning through my clothes, and realised that if I'd been paralysed, I probably wouldn't have been able to feel it. This was a big relief, although it was also quite uncomfortable. It had been a hot day – well, of course it'd been a hot day – and I had a strange sensation, just lying there in the middle of the road like that, of sunbathing. Not that anyone ever sunbathed any more, unless they had a death wish. Except, of course, the heat was coming up from beneath me instead of from above. Actually, it was probably more like being barbecued, or at least what I imagined it might be like. The car had hit me like a two-ton metal meat mallet and now there I was, all laid out on the griddle, sizzle sizzle, nice and tenderised. Any minute now I'd be just about done.

'Say, kid,' someone said, bending down over me, 'how do you feel?'

I thought that was a helluva question to ask someone who'd just been hit by a speeding car, and almost laughed right out loud. I *didn't*, but I almost did. I probably would have, though, except I thought it might not be such a great idea, under the circumstances. I thought I might cough up a lung or something.

'Just goddam peachy,' I replied, as ironical as it was possible to be, lying sprawled in the middle of the road like I was. I really laid it on. 'Thanks for asking.'

'Well,' he said, 'you look like crap.'

In case you've never noticed, some people are just filled with the milk of human kindness. They really are. It flows out of them like water out of a tap. It's enough to renew your faith in the whole human rat race. Although to be fair, I guess I might have taken the guy's question the wrong way in the first place, and then, after giving him such a snooty, wise-guy answer, maybe it wasn't so surprising that he gave me one straight back. I guess maybe I was in shock or something, which might have excused my manners, which are usually pretty good.

I mean, everywhere you look nowadays people are being treated for it – shock, that is, not good manners. It seems sometimes like you can't bump shopping trolleys at the grocery store without coming down with a case of it. I don't know, maybe people nowadays are just more shockable. What might have been mildly surprising twenty years ago seems like it can hospitalise a person today. So maybe that's what it was, maybe I was just in shock like everybody else. But I don't think so.

You know when you go to pick something up that you'd swear you'd just put down a second ago, and it's not there? And even when it turns up someplace else you're still not convinced it didn't just magically transport itself there just to perplex you? Well, that's kind of how I felt. Also a little embarrassed, to be honest. I mean, anyone would be, lying there spreadeagled in the middle of the road, with a whole bunch of strangers having a good old gawp at you, and thinking, 'Oh man, what if someone I know happens by?' and hoping you haven't pissed your pants.

Add to that the fact that *I* knew, and I knew that everyone *else* knew, I was a stupid retard who'd just stepped off the kerb into the path of a lousy speeding car.

And then I noticed a pretty young thing I'd seen around once or twice but never had the nerve to even smile at, and I just wished another car would come along and finish me off altogether.

4

'He stepped straight off the kerb in front of me! He must be crazy high on drugs or something! There oughta be a law against delinquents like him!'

The driver's concern for my welfare was heartwarming, it really was. He was being a real prince about it. Not that I blamed him or anything. In fact, I agreed with him. There ought to be a law against people like me. I mean it. I'd really done a terrific job on the front of his car, and it was a pretty nice model, too. I couldn't tell you what type it was, because I don't know the first thing about cars, but I remember it was white. I remember that because I remember lying on the ground and looking up at the front of it, which was dented all to hell, and expecting it to be all splattered with blood. My blood. But it wasn't. There wasn't a speck on it. And that's when I realised that, far from coughing up a lung, I hadn't even managed to cough up a little blood. Which, if I'd seen once, I must have seen a thousand times in one crummy movie or another. People in movies are forever coughing up blood. They can't get stabbed, or shot, or blown the hell up, or even, as in my case, just knocked the hell over by a speeding car, without doing it. It slowly gurgles up, like a spring, or a well that's just been tapped, and that's when you know whoever it is has had it. Of course, they're usually the main character's best friend, which is a positive death sentence in the movies, and they've usually just done something unbelievably heroic, or else unbelievably stupid. Either way, best friends nearly always get it in the neck. It's kind of a tradition. I guess if life was like the movies, and you were someone's best friend, you'd want to make sure whose story was being told before you decided whether to stick around or not. But then again, you'd have to be a real moron to believe the movies.

All the same, it didn't just happen on-screen. People bleeding all over the place, I mean. I once saw some goofy kid get well and truly creamed for real (although I couldn't tell you whether he was anyone's best friend or not). What happened was, one minute he was just sloping along, grinning his big fat head off, busy thinking whatever the hell it was he was busy thinking, and the next –

Splat –

He was jam.

5

'Did you see it? I saw the whole thing. *Pow!*'

'What sort of a person just steps off the kerb like that? What the hell is it with young people anyway?'

'Is he retarded? I've heard retards do it all the time.'

'Look at the front of my car, for Chrissakes! He's bent it all to hell!'

'The army'd soon straighten the little snot out! They'd soon knock him into shape!'

'Bring back conscription, I say!'

'Hey, don't I know you . . . ?' asked the pretty young thing I'd seen around once or twice, but never had the nerve to even smile at.

'*Jeezus Christ*! He's pissed his pants!'

6

To cut a long story short, there was quite a hullabaloo.

First the cops turned up, then an ambulance. More and more people stopped by to take a look. Pretty soon it was getting to be a regular sidewalk freak show. I probably should have held out a hat, I might've made a few bucks. But instead I just sort of lay there, right in the middle of everyone, the cops, and the ambulance guys, and the driver, and everybody who'd just stopped by to see the show, looking a bit dazed I guess, but still taking it all in. And that's when I began to notice that people were actually getting pretty hot under the collar.

'People like him shouldn't be allowed to walk the streets! Look what he's done to traffic flow!'

'Screw traffic flow! It's an abuse of valuable public resources, that's what it is! Police – ambulance – what next? The *fire* department?'

'And who's going to pay for it? I'll tell you who's going to pay for it. *Us!* The taxpayer!'

That's the trouble with people. They take everything so personally. Now, the driver I could understand. He was an interested party, and was sore for good reason. I mean, not only was the front of his car dented all to hell, but he probably had somewhere important to be. He was probably on his way to the opera or something. He wasn't *dressed* for the opera, but who the hell does nowadays, anyway. He was still having a rant to one of the cops, who I swear couldn't have been more than four feet tall. He wasn't a dwarf or anything, just really really small, more like a midget, and I remember thinking how well his uniform fitted. But the mood of the crowd in general was getting pretty ugly. And it was fast polarising into two distinct camps – those who thought I went about stepping off the kerb into the path of speeding cars for the fun of it, and those who thought I just didn't know any better.

'I don't care if he *is* a retard, he still oughta have his head examined!'

As I was being scooped up into the ambulance, I caught a flash of fist and heard a low grunt. By the time we pulled away, a riot chopper had arrived on the scene, johnny on the spot, and netted the lot of them.

7

I'd never ridden in the back of an ambulance before, so that was something. Of course, I would have preferred to be sitting up front, with the driver, as you got a better view, but it was still pretty interesting all the same. There was a lot of very interesting stuff to look at, too, even though I didn't really know what most of it was for. I tried to *imagine* what it was for, but I was probably wrong. You almost never can tell what medical equipment is for unless you've already seen someone use it, like on some dumb medical drama on television or something. And even then you don't know if that's how it's supposed to be used. I mean, when you see some actor playing a doctor, or a lawyer, or even a bus driver, you just tend to assume they know what they're doing, but I actually doubt it. It's probably just as confusing for them as it would be for you or me, plus they have to remember all that terrible dialogue. I mean, if you take a look at a tray of surgical instruments, all laid out nice and neat, ready for business, it's quite difficult to guess exactly what each one might be for. The same as when you're a little kid and you're taken to a fancy restaurant, or function or whatever, and the first course arrives, probably cold soup, and you look down and there's fifty different knives and forks and spoons to choose from. Well, of course you know you're supposed to use a spoon, at least, but the problem is, which one? Actually, when you think about it, it's not that complicated. You just work your way in from the outside. Maybe that's what doctors do, too. Just work their way in from the outside.

Anyway, I really had a good look around from where I was strapped down, craning my neck this way and that, checking everything out, and imagining what it might be used for, and what the chances were of them using it on me. It was a bit strange at first, being strapped down like that, but I guess it was for my own good. I guess they didn't want me rolling off the stretcher and onto the floor. They probably spent half their lives picking people up off the floor as it was, without the extra work of picking up people they'd already picked up once.

I don't know why, but I was more curious about everything than I was concerned. About my health, I mean. I probably should have been concerned, I know, but I wasn't. People up to a certain age aren't, I think, and then, after a certain age, that's just about all they *are* concerned about. But even though I wasn't, I thought I'd enter into the spirit of the thing, just for the fun of it, and imagine that I was. It was too dramatic an opportunity to waste, so what I did was, I started imagining I was being rushed to hospital for an urgent, life-saving, very risky operation. So risky was it, in fact, that it had never even been attempted before, and so urgent that I'd probably be dead before they got me onto the operating table anyway. By the time I was finished, I'd even conjured up a loved one, leaning over me clutching my hand and telling me that everything was going to be just fine, I'd see, with me going along for the ride, saying yeah, course it was, even though we both knew I was a dead duck. But then I started getting a lump in my throat just thinking about it, so I quit it. The last thing I needed was to start blubbing just because of my stupid imagination.

Then, to take my mind off trying not to blub, I thought I'd try to start up a little conversation.

'Say, this looks like a pretty interesting job,' I said to the ambulance guys, as they fussed about, checking my vitals, and so on. They were really doing a first-rate job. Very professional. 'How would a person go about becoming an ambulance guy, anyway? You know, if they were considering that kind of a career, for instance.'

I wasn't really considering it, of course. I was just making conversation. I thought it was only polite considering all the trouble they were taking. And besides, apart from trying to take my mind off trying not to blub, at times I'm a regular conversation maniac. I can't help it. Sometimes you just can't shut me up. Like at bus stops. People have even caught the wrong bus just to get away from me. I mean, it might even be going in the opposite direction and everything. It might not even be *stopping*. Once I get started, sometimes there's just no stopping me. But then, at other times, I can't stand it. Someone'll try to strike up a conversation with me and I might as well have a couple of earfuls of wet cement for all the interest I'll show. Like when I'm getting my hair cut, for instance. I just hate it when barbers talk to you, and I haven't even got anything against barbers. I mean, if I met my barber outside or at Moriarty's or someplace, I could talk to him all day. I'd enjoy it.

But then I thought of something that was actually a

17

pretty interesting observation, and was all the more interesting because it had never occurred to me before. 'Say,' I said again, I don't know why, it was just a habit I seemed to have got into, talking with those damn talkative ambulance guys, 'don't you think it's kind of funny how little kids always want to be bus drivers and firemen, but you never hear of a kid who wants to be an ambulance driver? Don't you think that's kind of funny? Why do you think that is? I mean, do you have any opinion on the subject?'

It was a pretty good question, even if I do say so myself. Not exactly profound, maybe, but interesting. Personally, I never wanted to be either, but I'd certainly known kids who did. Certain kids I knew never wanted to be anything *but* bus drivers or firemen, like they were the two most glamorous professions in the world or something. But the two ambulance guys just kind of looked at me, like maybe they were thinking, 'Concussion,' or maybe even, 'Brain damage.' They really were two talkative sonsuvbitches, that's for sure, but I thought I might as well stick with it now that I'd started, so I said, 'I mean, it's gotta be more exciting than driving a bus, don't you agree? For one thing, you've got a siren. That's like having a licence to scare the hell out of people. And for another, you can drive just about anywhere you goddam want to – over the sidewalk, up one-way streets, through red lights. Goddam anywhere.'

It was true, too. Ambulance drivers ruled the roads. Even police cars gave way to them, sometimes. The only thing an ambulance had to give way to, I guess, was another ambulance, although I don't know in that case how they decided who had priority. Anyway, we were probably speeding through a set of red lights or up a one-way street even as I spoke, judging by the sudden screech of brakes and ear-splitting *CRASH* we left in our wake. I thought I could even hear a hubcap bouncing down the road.

I whistled. 'Man,' I said, 'that sounded pretty bad. Say, shouldn't we stop or something? You know, to help. I mean, I don't mind or anything. In fact, I'd be glad of the company.'

But the ambulance guys obviously weren't interested in making small talk. Or in stopping. I guess they'd heard and seen it all before.

I decided to take a different tack.

'So,' I asked them, suddenly all matter-of-fact, like I was the kind of guy who preferred to have it straight, no punches pulled, no matter what the prognosis, 'am I gonna make it?'

8

I'd like to have seen their faces. My parents, I mean, when they got the call from the hospital telling them that their retarded offspring had apparently stepped off the kerb into the path of a speeding car without suffering so much as a nosebleed and was being held under observation. They'd have been as sore as a couple of three-day-old boils. That's what they do in hospitals when they can't make up their minds what's wrong with you, by the way. Hold you under observation. Some people have been under observation for years. They just sit in their hospital beds being observed, sometimes round the clock. Of course, sometimes they go crazy, and then they don't have to be observed any more because the doctors know what's wrong with them. Other times the doctors go crazy.

Naturally I was all for getting out of there asagp (as soon as goddam possible), but the doctors had other ideas. I don't know if it was just them being conscientious, or whether they only wanted to keep me there long enough to get the chance to show the hell off in front of my parents. Probably they just wanted the chance to show the hell off, because I noticed they always kept one eye on the door, just so they'd know the instant they turned up. The reason they may or may not have wanted to show off was because my father's a bit of a big shot, to tell you the truth. A real big deal. I'm not going to tell you what he does or anything, if you don't already know. If you ever meet him I'm sure he'll be delighted to tell you himself, though. And my mother, apparently, used to be some kind of famous beauty or something. Apparently she could have made a fortune modelling or in the movies or whatever, except she couldn't even be bothered. But anyway, they confiscated all my clothes and gave me a smock to wear, figuring I'd probably be too embarrassed to try and escape. They were right too. And then for the next two hours I couldn't turn around without being poked or prodded or tested for something or other, which can really try a person's patience.

'Hey, cut it out,' I told one of them at last, after he'd crept up behind me and jabbed me right in the ribs. I guess he wanted to make double sure they weren't busted or something. Anyway, he surprised me by giving a big, fat guffaw, like I'd just made a terrific joke.

'Hey, that's a good one, kid,' he said. 'Hey, did you hear what the kid just said? He told me to cut it out!' All the other doctors, and the nurses too, thought this was hilarious, and gave big, fat guffaws as well. Then I saw what he meant. I'd just given him a joke he'd probably still be wheeling out in fifty years' time, which I really resented because I really can't stand doctors, especially wisecracking ones using my material. I mean, it's a noble profession and all, but I just can't stand them. Partly it's because they're usually terrifically smug, which I find a very unattractive character trait, and partly it's the thought of them being able to carve me up without even needing to follow the dotted lines.

When my parents did finally arrive, after about five hours, all the doctors and nurses bustled around trying to look more professional than each other, but at the same time trying to get a good look at them, too. It wouldn't have surprised me a bit if one or two of them had pulled out an autograph book. That wouldn't have surprised me at all. It wouldn't have surprised me if my mother or father had signed it, either. I was used to it, though. I'd seen it thousands of times. I just pretended I wasn't even there. I might have tried jumping out a window, except we were a couple of floors up and I was wearing that damn smock.

'I'm afraid your son has had a very lucky escape,' a particularly smug-faced doctor, who'd managed to elbow his way to the front of the scrum, informed my purse-lipped parents.

Boy, I loved that. He was *afraid* I'd had a lucky escape. I thought that was priceless, and guffawed right out loud. It was hysterical. The guy should have been a comedian – that, or else given a good slap. But my parents didn't seem to get the joke. When I let out that big guffaw, they both just looked at me like I was nuts. Like maybe I'd just fallen out of a mental institution, right at their feet. They probably thought I'd landed on my head. Maybe I did.

'He can count himself a very lucky young man indeed.'

There he goes again. '*Lucky?*' I thought. 'You smug sonuvabitch.' Boy, I hate it when people say things like that. That's just the kind of smug behaviour I was talking about. I felt like sticking a scalpel in his neck and seeing how lucky *he* felt. 'As far as *I'm* concerned,'

I felt like telling him, once I'd stabbed him with his own scalpel, '*not* getting hit by a car would've been lucky. What *would* have been lucky is if instead of getting hit by a car I'd found fifty bucks on the sidewalk. *That* would've been lucky.'

That's what I *felt* like telling him. I didn't, though. I couldn't even be bothered. But if he'd been looking for a pat on the back he must have been pretty disappointed. I know most parents probably lap stuff like that up, about their kids narrowly escaping death or whatever, but not mine. They both still looked like they were sucking lemons or something. Like they did when there wasn't enough gin in their gin. Actually, you might have thought the whole situation, with or without the smug comments, might have elicited at least a twinge of parental emotion. Nothing too over the top or dramatic, I don't mean. No actual histrionics or anything undignified like that. I just mean some kind of show of relief, maybe, or gratitude, or anger even. But you'd be wrong. Although to be fair, emotions had never really been their big thing, so I didn't take it personally or anything. Some people can't ever learn to ride a bike, or to chew with their mouths shut either. They just never get the hang of it. Besides, my mother could, on occasion, come over all parental, but only if she was in the right mood. Today, though, the most she could manage was a pretty lame 'Oh, really?' while my horny father finally stopped sucking on his imaginary lemon long enough to eye up a cute nurse who was managing to put a remarkable amount of wiggle into the back end of her uniform.

At least he had pretty good taste, I'll say that for him. And at least they didn't leave me there as some kind of lousy guinea pig, with my ass hanging out, although it must have been tempting.

9

The trip home in the car went something like this:

My father: I hate this city. It's full of freaks! No wonder people are moving out in droves.

My mother: (gazing absently out the window) Are they? I hadn't noticed.

My father: Of course they are! Haven't you noticed all the empty buildings? The city's full of them!

My mother: Full of them? I thought you said it was empty.

My father: Full of empty buildings! The city's full of empty buildings. And freaks.

My mother: Freaks?

My father: They're moving into all the empty buildings.

My mother: Are they? I hadn't noticed.

My father: Ah, that's the genius of it! They've learnt to blend in. It's now almost impossible to tell the freaks from the non-freaks.

My mother: Then how do you know who's moving in and who's moving out?

My father: It's not easy.

That's the way conversations generally went, not just in the car, either, which might have been all right, but all the time. The thing is, my parents are almost certainly out of their minds. I used to wonder, when I was younger, 'What the hell are they talking about?' I mean, I really didn't have a clue. Once I even asked them. I just came right out and said, 'What the hell are you talking about? I haven't understood a single goddam word.' They both just stared at me like I was some kind of talking rock. They didn't know what the hell *I* was talking about. They didn't have a clue.

My father actually had a bit of a thing about freaks. I guess you'd call it a hang-up. I was never too sure though about who qualified. I mean, who was or wasn't one. He never actually pointed one out to me in the street or anything ('Look, son – over there. A freak!') so I never really knew what to look for. As far as I understood it, though, they could be just about anyone, anywhere, moving around amongst us without us even knowing it, impersonating ordinary decent citizens, riding the subway and collecting their laundry, like something out of some old propaganda movie. Like those old communists everyone used to get so worked up about. But I didn't worry about it too much. I finally decided I'd probably just know one when I saw one.

I don't know if it's particularly unusual, but I don't even know how my parents met. Of course I know my mother was this famous beauty and all, and my father some highly eligible big shot, but they could've met down a mineshaft for all I know, or been stranded on a desert island. Looking at them now, you'd think there weren't enough coincidences in the world to get them together, but I guess they did, somehow. Somehow I guess they met and fell in love and decided to get married just like everybody else does, like people do every day. Like people have done every day for thousands of years (think of that!). Somehow, though, I just couldn't imagine it. I tried to, but it was no good. I also used to wonder what they might have been like when they were my age, before they even met, but I eventually gave that up too. It was starting to give me headaches. I guess thinking about some things will do that to you.

I guess what I'm trying to say is we weren't really that close. We weren't the kind of family that sits around gasbagging about our day and stuff like that. You know, like some corny family on some corny old TV show where everybody sits around the table making terrifically witty small talk, even really young kids, and everyone's extremely interested in every little thing everyone else has done or said since the last time they were sitting round the table, which was probably at breakfast over flapjacks or maybe even waffles. I don't know if there ever were any real-life families like that, but I guess if there were, then maybe there still are, somewhere. Who knows. What I do know is that if we'd ever tried it I wouldn't have been a bit surprised if we actually bored each other's heads clean off. I really wouldn't.

'How was your day, son?'

'Great, Dad! I was knocked down by a speeding car and pissed my pants.'

Thump! (goes his head).

'Oh, too bad! Wait'll I tell you about my day.'

Thump! (goes mine).

In fact, we were no sooner through the door than my mother came down with one of her 'heads', and presumably went off to change it. She had a couple of bolts in her neck and a whole closet full of spares.

My father promptly disappeared into his den.

Boy, my father and his den. That den, and what he did in it, was some big mystery. In all my life I'd never so much as caught a peek inside it, but the funny thing was, I wasn't even the least bit curious. You might think I would have been, but I wasn't. He could have had a performing albino elephant in there for all I knew, and I couldn't have cared a damn. Of course, one of my earliest memories is actually of my father sitting me down, man to man, and telling me, 'Whatever else you do, son, keep the hell out of my den.' I guess that kind of thing can either spark a kid's curiosity, or else kill it stone dead.

Rather than rattle round the old mausoleum, which could be as depressing as hell, I went straight to my room, and swiped my way in. But first I had to pass wall upon wall of the crummiest pictures you've ever seen. I mean it. They were so crummy, most of them, I can't even begin to describe them. My parents must have had the lousiest taste in art of just about anyone in the whole world, but of course, they didn't think that. They thought they were real connoisseurs. People with really lousy taste often think that. And to make it even worse, some of them were as big as the wall they were hanging on! They were enormous! Boy, just looking at them made me depressed. And it wasn't even as if the subject matter was uniformly depressing or anything. In fact, just the opposite. They were so goddam chirpy, some of them, they made me want to bang my head against a wall.

10

My room was a mess, of course. I'd been toying with the idea of tidying up a bit, but in the end I couldn't see the point. I find it pretty easy to be philosophical about stuff like that. The door snapped shut behind me, and I threw myself on the bed, which was still covered with all sorts of junk I'd been playing with earlier, like some books, a baseball glove, a magnifying glass and this beautiful kaleidoscope I've had since I was a kid. Now that I thought about it, it'd been a heckuva long day. Some days are like that. They feel like they're about a year long. Then what I did was I just stared at the ceiling. I can usually do this for hours, and often do. It's sort of a talent I have. Of course, as far as talents go, I know it's not particularly impressive or anything, but I can't tell you how much enjoyment I get out of it, just lying there, staring at it, mind blank. I actually think everyone would benefit tremendously if they spent at least part of each day doing the same thing. I don't mean they'd have to actually lie down and stare at a ceiling for hours. They could stare at a ceiling, a wall, a tree, whatever, and for however long they felt like. I really find it very soothing, and I'm sure a lot of other people would, too. But for some reason, after only about two minutes I was bored, which is very unusual for me, as I hardly ever get bored. I think I've already mentioned how I've got a very low pain threshold. Well, I've also got what I guess you might call a very high boredom threshold. So then I just switched on the television instead. I can't stand television. There are some things I can't stand that sometimes when I do them I can't quite remember exactly what it was about them I couldn't stand, but not television. Every time I watch TV I remember exactly why I can't stand it. I still watch it, sometimes, though. I don't know why.

The wars weren't going well, as usual. Not that anyone noticed any more. Or cared. It had been a couple of years now since some genius had come up with the idea of turning them into round-the-clock entertainment, and since then it had become pretty much irrelevant who was winning or losing, as long as it rated through the roof. Which it did. Now the sponsors had moved in, and the production values had gone all Hollywood. It was even starting to attract some pretty big names. Film stars were lining up to go to war because no one was going to the movies any more.

Anyway, I must've clicked through a couple of hundred channels before I came across something interesting, an old horror movie starring Boris Karloff and some creaky old sets. It must have been a hundred years old, but I just love that stuff, so I dimmed the lights down low for atmosphere, snuggled back into my pillows and just lay there, staring up at the flickering old film. But then, I don't know why, I started thinking about things, and in particular about the girl by the side of the road, the one I'd seen around once or twice and hadn't even had the nerve to smile at. I don't know what it was, but there was something about her that I found very intriguing. She looked like a very interesting person. I thought I

30

really wouldn't mind getting to know her better. But then something terrible occurred to me. I don't know why I hadn't thought of it before. 'Oh man,' I thought, 'I really hope she didn't get netted along with the rest of them.' That would've been too bad. I'd heard bad things about what happened to people who got picked up like that. I'd heard they were dropped right in the Hudson. I didn't believe it, though.

11

I hardly ever dream. That is, I know I must, because I read somewhere or other that everyone does, all the time apparently. Apparently it's like a midnight movie marathon inside our heads while we're sleeping, except some people – like me, for instance – can't seem to remember any of the plots or the characters, and without even a ticket stub to hang on to, they wake up in the morning and think they haven't been dreaming, when they have. I guess one day there'll be a machine to record your dreams, so you'll be able to watch them back just like home movies. I guess people like me will be the first in line to snap them up.

Whether I usually dream or not, though, that night I definitely did. I dreamed of a clown, of all things, just like the ones I once saw when I was a kid. I know other people talking about their dreams is boring as hell. I know it. In fact, when someone starts up telling me about some dream they've had, I feel like saying, 'Stop right there. I know you probably think it's terrifically interesting and everything, and maybe it is. But the thing is, I'm just not interested.' I don't say it, of course, but I definitely feel like saying it. And even after whoever it is has told me their dream – because I was too cowardly to tell them I wasn't interested in the first place – and even if the dream *was* terrifically interesting – nine times out of ten, I'll guarantee you, it'll have been boring all

32

the same. Which in itself is kind of interesting, because if it was a book or a movie the person was telling you about, or something that actually happened to them, it probably would be interesting. But anyway, I must have only been about five or six when I saw them that one time. Even back then, though, I wasn't too crazy about clowns. I thought it was a very dubious way to make a living, if you want to know the truth, even back then. Also, I was pretty embarrassed for everyone else in the audience, my parents included. The way they were all nearly busting a gut laughing, you'd have thought it was the funniest thing they'd ever seen in their lives. I remember thinking people were going to be sick. *Actually* be sick. I don't know why, but I didn't find it funny at all. At first I just found it embarrassing, but then it started to get alarming. Not the clowns themselves, which I know some people think are kind of spooky anyway, but everybody laughing their heads off at them. Looking at everybody, I suddenly had the idea that the whole world must have gone mad, everybody except me. I really thought everyone had gone insane. The really alarming thing, though, the really terrifying part, was that I wasn't insane too. That nearly scared the pants off me. I wanted to be, but I just wasn't. And now, after all these years, I was dreaming about one. I didn't find him any funnier, either. He was wearing a pair of big old floppy clown shoes, which made a fat wet slapping sound every time he took a step, like smacking the side-walk with a fish, and he was holding a big balloon by a piece of string, which just hung above his head. But the strange thing was I didn't get the impression it was lighter than air, even though it was hanging above his head like that. In fact, I got just the opposite impression. It looked grey and solid and heavy as lead, and hung up there like some affront to gravity.

To make matters worse, he didn't say a word, he just stood there grinning from ear to ear. But of course he wasn't really grinning at all, not really, he was just giving the impression he was grinning, because he had a grin as wide as the Grand Canyon greasepainted across his crazy ugly clown face.

Behind that grin his face was like a brick wall.

12

In the morning when I awoke I felt, to be honest with you, not exactly one hundred per cent in the pink. I felt like I'd been through a grinder, a meat mincer or something, and then reshaped from a lump of raw, shredded mince. I felt tender all over, like one big, black bruise. I felt terrible. I still dragged myself out of bed, though. I thought I'd better take a look in the mirror.

I didn't really like looking at myself in the mirror, but I did anyway. I know some guys who can stare at themselves all day long and never get sick of the sight of their own backside. And the thing is, they're not even the least bit embarrassed about it, either, even if other people are around. To see them doing it, you'd think they were Rudolph Valentino or somebody. Or Errol Flynn. Every time they see a mirror they're at it. When I see guys like that in bathrooms or in elevators or somewhere I feel like telling them, 'You're so beautiful I can't stand it.' I really do. Of course, they're the same kind of guys who at any given time know every single item of clothing they've got on, right down to their underwear. Ask them what colour jocks they're wearing and I swear they could tell you. Personally, I'm pretty suspicious of people like that.

Not that I'm a complete slob or anything. I don't mean that. If anything, I'm probably considered well-dressed. That is, I wear nice clothes, but I just throw them on any old how. And I'm not so repulsive that I don't want to look in a mirror because I don't want to be reminded of it. It's just that I'm not entirely convinced, when I do look in one, that what I see in there is really me. Of course, I know it *looks* like me. I'm not saying that. I know it's how I look and everything. But it's more like staring at some stranger or somebody who just happens to look exactly like me, and I keep half expecting him to make some rude gesture or other, the same as if I was caught out staring at somebody on a bus or somewhere.

But as I say, I gave myself the quick once-over all the same, in the buff and all. I thought, feeling the way I did, I was sure to be half black and blue, at least. I was ready for the worst. But I wasn't. In fact, there wasn't so much as a dent or a bruise on me. Not a scratch. On the contrary, my reflection appeared sleek and healthy and remarkably unmarked, and in the process of my examination, I couldn't help but notice, and even admire, the direction my still boyish body was taking.

It was definitely burgeoning, still smooth but suddenly hard.

And then, a little embarrassed, I pulled on some clothes and went downstairs, where I found Louie Louie eating my breakfast.

13

I greeted him with a friendly 'Louie Louie, you goddam pig!' which surprised the hell out of him, and then nearly made him choke on the huge mouthful of bacon and eggs he'd just been shovelling into his fat face. I even had to thump him on the back a couple of times before it came out again in a disgusting half-masticated lump, and just sat there on the side of his plate. Or rather, my plate. Actually, I really shouldn't have distracted him like that while he was eating as there was a long history of blocked windpipes in his family. They were always choking on some damn thing or other. It was like a family curse or something.

'You nearly made me choke!' he gasped, looking up at me with pink, watery eyes, once the danger had passed.

I sat down at the other side of the table. I put my feet up on a chair and relaxed.

'You should learn to chew your food, Louie Louie, that's your problem,' I told him, and poured myself a cup of coffee. I was already starting to feel a lot better. 'But then I guess that comes from sharing a trough with all those other little piggy-wiggies.'

This wasn't the least bit personal, you understand, it was just the way we talked to one another. Besides, you could hit old Louie Louie over the head with a baseball bat and he wouldn't take it personally. In fact, he was grinning like a real sonuvabitch. He was just about the grinniest sonuvabitch that ever lived.

'So,' he said, still grinning but also continuing to shovel food into his already full mouth like if he stopped he'd instantly die of starvation. He had a very big appetite. He would've already had one breakfast at his house, at least. It's not like his parents starved him or anything. 'What's this about you stepping off the kerb into the path of a goddam speeding car, huh? What are you, some kind of retard or something?'

Good news sure travelled fast. And I was already getting sick of the retard angle. I thought I'd better try and nip it in the bud.

'The car was out of control!' I protested shrilly. I was trying for just the right note of righteous indignation, but I guess I probably failed. I'm a terrible actor, unlike Louie Louie. 'A pedestrian isn't safe in this crummy city any more. The driver must've been crazy high on drugs or something. Or late for the lousy opera.' I'd already put a couple of sugars in my coffee, but I put another couple in anyway. I felt I needed it.

But Louie Louie just sat there looking smug and playing with the disgusting half-masticated lump of breakfast he'd regurgitated. He'd already just about licked the plate clean, and I just knew he was going to eat that, too. I knew he was going to eat it because when you know someone really well you just know when they'll do something even really disgusting, like eat some half-masticated breakfast they've just coughed up. Actually, it's pretty funny the disgusting things people will do without even realising it. Take a look around you. There are people out there doing some pretty disgusting stuff, and I bet if you were to go up to them and just casually tap them on the shoulder and actually point out to them just how disgusting it is, they'd quite possibly turn around and thank you. That, or else sock you on the jaw.

'Well,' he said, finally popping the disgusting dollop into his mouth, just like I knew he would, 'that's not what I heard.'

I racked my brain. I could imagine *what* he'd heard, but I couldn't think who he might have heard it from. Trust Louie Louie, though. He had contacts everywhere, I guess because he was such an amiable person. He'd talk to just about anyone. Old ladies, bums, anyone. He wasn't moody like me. I can be terrifically moody at times. Anyway, there was nothing for it but to ask.

'And what exactly *did* you hear, and from *whom*, pray tell?' I said it with as much affectation as I could muster, just for the hell of it, and in this very posh, English accent, even though I stink at accents. I also did it to cover my embarrassment, I guess, because I was still quite embarrassed about the whole episode.

'I heard you stepped off the kerb into the path of a goddam speeding car,' said Louie Louie, his big fat grin spreading across his big fat breakfast-smeared face, 'and I believe I was reliably informed.'

I thumped the table, making my coffee spill. 'By *whom*?' I demanded, all bluff and bluster, like I was in some terrible play or something. 'Supply me with a name, you breakfast-scoffing scoundrel!'

Louie Louie liked that. He was smiling his damn head off. Then he told me. I probably should have

39

guessed, but I didn't. I can be very slow sometimes. I admit it.

'Some sweet little cutie who was there, johnny on the spot,' he said. 'Saw the whole goddam thing.'

POW!

14

It had to be the same girl, I was sure of it. It was a big relief, too, knowing she hadn't been dumped in the river after all. I'd felt pretty guilty about that. I figured the rest of the ghouls probably had it coming, what with their smart comments and everything, but I was pleased she'd managed to get away. I was also rather curious about one or two things all of a sudden, now that I knew who'd told Louie Louie all about it. There were definitely a number of things I was quite interested in finding out.

Actually, what I was most curious about was whether or not she'd slipped away before that lousy loudmouth blurted out about my having pissed my pants. That was my chief priority. Of course, I couldn't come right out and ask, though. That would be a huge mistake. That sort of thing is just the sort of thing a person likes to keep close to their chest, for obvious reasons. Plus Louie Louie was probably a bigger loudmouth than the bastard who'd said it. He couldn't keep a secret if his life depended on it. So what I did was I decided to grill him about one or two other matters instead, but in a deceptively cool, casual manner, like I was only asking for something to do. Because I was bored or something. The last thing you want to do when getting any information out of Louie Louie is to give him the impression you're interested. If you do that, you've had it.

'So,' I said, as if I was making conversation for the hell of it, you know, like I was so bored I was about to fall off my chair. Like I said, though, I'm a terrible actor. 'Howdja come to know her, anyway?'

Louie Louie let out a terrific belch.

'Know who?' he said.

'Whoever it was told you.'

'Oh,' he said. 'Her.'

'Yeah,' *I* said. 'Her.'

That's when he started picking his teeth with a fingernail. He was very thorough about it too. He was determined to do a good job. Then when he'd dislodge something, what he'd do is he'd eat it. He was very methodical and thorough about this as well. Of course, I guess I could have tapped him on the shoulder like I was just saying and pointed out how disgusting it was, but it wouldn't have done any good. It really wouldn't.

Finally, after about an hour, it looked like he was finished. Of course, it wasn't really an hour, but watching somebody pick their teeth for two minutes *feels* like an hour. But he wasn't finished after all. He started up again. Then he said, 'Wuddaya wanna know for?' but while he was still delving around inside his mouth. He really had beautiful manners. You could take him anywhere.

'No reason,' I told him. Boy, was I being casual about it.

He had something stuck in a back tooth now and really had to concentrate. It must have been really wedged in there, because he had to get half his hand in to try and get it out. I thought about offering him a pair of pliers or something. When he finally managed to extract it he held it up for examination. It looked like a piece of bacon rind, but he was examining it like it was some rare and exotic artefact he'd just unearthed. I don't know what else he'd expected to find in there.

'From around,' he said at long last, finally getting round to answering my original question.

Boy, I really hate answers like that. Whenever I hear someone give an answer like that I always feel like knocking their head against the nearest hard surface. I feel like knocking their stupid brains out.

'Well,' I said, instead of doing what I wanted to do, which was bang his head against the tabletop, 'howdja come to be talking to her, anyway?'

Now he yawned so wide I thought his head was going to crack in two. It was just about the phoniest yawn I'd ever seen in my life. He didn't cover his mouth with his hand or anything either. 'I guess we just sorta bumped into one another,' he drawled, once he'd finished pretending to yawn his fat head off. 'You know.'

I didn't, but I kind of pretended to lose interest here. I was being very tactical. I took a mouthful of coffee, and then I just started humming a bit of that same tune that'd been going round my head lately – 'I've Got My Love to Keep Me Warm' – that not even a goddam speeding car could dislodge. There was always some tune or other going round in there. Sometimes the only way to get rid of it was to find another tune. Then, after about a minute or so, I tried again. A tactical advance.

'So,' I said, even more casually this time, like it was just about the last thing I was actually interested in, 'what's she like?'

It was a mistake, though. He was onto it in a second.

'*Like?*'

Damn!

Time to retreat. Get the hell out of there. 'I mean . . .' – what kind of a stupid, moronic question was that to ask? What was I thinking? Boy, what a dummy – 'I mean,' I babbled, desperately tying to think of some way to unsay what I'd just said, 'what's her opinion, for example, on the whole retard angle, etc? I mean – does she have one?'

But Louie Louie just looked across the table at me. I really didn't like the look of that look, either. It made me very uncomfortable, like I was pretending it wasn't my feet that smelled when it was. He didn't say anything, though. He didn't need to. After a while I couldn't stand it any more and just cracked. I'm lousy at poker too, and I'd be terrible under torture. I'd rat out anyone in two seconds.

'*What?*' I demanded, but Louie Louie just shook his head as if I was the personification of all human folly or something, and he was suddenly Louie Louie the Wise. I almost wished I'd let him choke when I had the chance.

'Either you landed on your head, Montanna,' he said at last, like he was making some terrifically profound pronouncement, 'or else you've got it pretty bad.'

He was right, too. One way or the other.

'Wuddaya goddam mean?' I demanded, although of course I already knew exactly what he meant. I was as touchy as dammit. I admit it.

'I *mean*,' he repeated, nice and slow, like he really was talking to a retard, 'either – you – landed – on – your – god – dam – *head* – or – else – you've – got it – pre – tty – god – dam – *bad*.'

The thing is, he had a point. Which was not only rare, but extremely annoying. I did have it pretty bad. It's true. Otherwise what was with all the questions? After all, I didn't even know the girl. Sure, I'd seen her around once or twice, and thought she was cute and looked kind of interesting, but that was it. The city was full of cute girls, and *some* of them, at *least*, had to be kind of interesting too. And yet there I was carrying on like some lovesick dummy over this one girl in particular. And I wasn't even the type. You know, chocolates and flowers and all that phoney crap. That kind of thing usually made me laugh my pants off. It made me want to be ill on the spot. Not that I couldn't be as sentimental as the next guy, you understand. I could. It's just that I knew where to draw a dignified line. I had my pride. My self-respect.

'Okay, you lousy, no-good, sadistic sonuvabitch,' I told him. 'You're right. I admit it. Maybe I have got it bad. Maybe I even landed on my goddam head. Happy? Now cough it up, why don'tcha. What's her name?'

Oh boy, old Louie Louie just loved that. He'd won hands down. I'd cracked like an egg. His day really couldn't have been working out any better if he'd planned it. Which he probably did.

'Sunday Daffodil,' he said, and just grinned his big fat head off some more. 'Her name's Sunday Daffodil, for Chrissakes.'

15

You have to admit it was a helluva name. Actually, I'm pretty reluctant to say what it is I'm about to say because I know it's going to sound as corny as hell, and when you hear what it is you'll know what I mean. But the thing is, sometimes you've just got to come right out with that kind of stuff without really thinking about it, because once you start wondering about just how corny it's going to sound to someone else, you're never going to say it. Anyway, what I wanted to say was this.

It sounded like music.

Her name, I mean. Of course, I didn't say this out loud or anything. That's exactly the kind of thing you don't go around saying out loud. Going around saying that kind of thing's never done anyone's reputation any good, that's for sure. It was worrying enough just thinking it. But even without me saying it, Louie Louie just sat there looking very amused and superior about the whole thing, which is easy to do I guess when your best friend has suddenly gone all soft in the head over some girl he doesn't even know but you do. You can afford to be all superior about a thing like that.

'Montanna,' he said, 'you oughta take a look at yourself in a mirror. I'm not kidding. You look like you've just heard angels or something.'

It's funny, but it was a pretty perceptive thing to say, especially for Louie Louie. In a corny kind of way, I *had* just heard something heavenly.

16

Apart from being a real regular pain in the side, as I've mentioned, and making the extremely rare perceptive observation, Louie Louie was also the kind of guy who would ogle his best friend's mother right in front of him and not think anything of it. This is exactly what he did now, right under my own nose, with Sunday Daffodil's name still chiming sweetly in the air. I guess that sort of thing should have made me pretty mad, but to be fair, my mother didn't exactly leave much to the imagination. I mean, sometimes she dressed quite provocatively, especially for an older woman. It depended on her mood.

She was a strange fish, that's for sure. She could tear a hole in the *Titanic* one day, she was so icy, and then be all girly and flirtatious the next. Also, she was highly medicated (of course, so was half the goddam country). But she loved an audience, when she was in the right mood. Any audience. Maybe she regretted not being in the movies after all, and was determined to grab whatever attention there was left to grab, even if it was only old Louie Louie's or whoever's. I mean, she would come swanning in half naked, sloshing her favourite bubbling potion round its cut-glass beaker, fully aware I had company, and then make some lame attempt at covering herself up while Louie Louie or whoever it was would just sit there ogling away like crazy. It was pathetic really.

I know once upon a time she was some famous beauty and everything, but about a hundred years ago, and that kind of thing can get a little embarrassing, especially with people drooling all over the furniture. Yet as embarrassing as it was, for some reason I never had the heart to tell Louie Louie or whoever it was to quit it. Or rather, I guess I knew my mother got some queer kind of kick out of it, and who was I to deprive her of a little fun, anyway? Being married to my father couldn't exactly have been terrifically entertaining.

Today she must have woken up all girly and flirtatious, I guess, because she came gliding in half wearing some sheer little satin trifle of a nightdress and a pair of fluffy pumps. *Pumps*, for Chrissake. I knew she was there before I'd even seen her because I saw Louie Louie's eyes nearly pop out of his head. When she saw the two of us sitting there at the breakfast table she pretended to be as surprised as hell.

'Why, *good*ness!' she exclaimed, laying it on with the same trowel she used for her make-up. 'I didn't know we had *comp*any!'

Boy, oh boy, she was some big fat double phoney. I say 'double phoney' because not only was she fully aware we had company, but because she never usually used words like 'goodness' when she could use a 'goddam' instead.

'*Field*ing, you *terr*ible boy! You should have *told* me, for goodness' sake!'

(There she goes again. What a performer.)

Then she turned her attention to Louie Louie. He went right on ogling her, though, just a little more tactfully. He couldn't take his eyes off her. It was embarrassing.

'Why, Louie Louie,' she continued, on a real roll now, 'just look at you. I swear you're more handsome and grown up every time I see you. I do declare, you'll be *shaving* next!' You'd think she was Scarlett O'Hara or somebody by the way she was talking, but she was actually from Buffalo.

'Already am, Mrs Montanna. Shaved twice just last week.'

The goddam liar. 'You liar,' I told him.

'Did too. Heavy beards run in my family.'

'Only on your mother's side.'

'Now, now, Fielding, dear. Be nice. It's not Louie Louie's fault if he's mature for his age. I'm sure you'll catch up in time.'

I wouldn't ordinarily have let it get to me. I was used to it. And I knew before I'd even done what it was I was about to do that I shouldn't do it, but I just couldn't help myself. I suppose it might have been Louie Louie jiggling imaginary breasts at me behind her back, but I don't think so. I think it was just me feeling suddenly sore towards the world in general, which happens. Anyway, what I did was I started to mouth something as if I was really talking. I did it very naturally, not overdoing it, until my mother started tapping the back of her ear and said, 'What was that, darling? I didn't quite catch it.'

'I said, maybe you need to turn up your hearing aid.'

That was all I said, but it was a lousy thing to do. I know it. Particularly as she actually wore a hearing aid for real. Except it wasn't really a hearing aid, more a bionic ear or something from when some ambassador or other's wife had bitten off her real one in a fit of pique. She'd busted the other one years earlier in a hunting accident. Whatever it was, she was a bit sensitive about it, and I really shouldn't have been so crass as to mention it in company. As soon as I'd done it, I wished I hadn't.

Anyway, there was this very sudden change in mood, and nobody said anything. I could've apologised, I guess, but I didn't. I'm very childish like that. Instead, Louie Louie and I just sat there, while my mother, even though she was still standing there half naked in her negligee and pumps, looked like she'd just had all the wind knocked out of her sails. She looked like she'd been punched in the stomach. Sometimes it only takes a little thing to make someone feel like that. The worst thing is, I knew just what it was. Hell, it was a low-down shoddy trick and I was sorry, I truly was, but just then Louie Louie opened up his big fat trap and said, 'Hearing aid or not, I think you're a goddam knockout, Mrs Montanna!'

Boy, when he said that I swear I could've gutted him with a spoon.

17

After that, I just about dragged Louie Louie out of the house. I didn't even bother combing my hair or anything. When we were safely outside I tried smoothing it back, but it wouldn't do it. It refused. I didn't care, though. To be honest, I was just glad to be outside, I felt so lousy all of a sudden. All of a sudden, I felt so lousy I could've thrown myself under a bus. Of course, I was just feeling bad about what I'd said, and sore at Louie Louie for what *he'd* said, even though he'd only said it to make up for what I'd said in the first place, but I still felt like throwing myself under a bus all the same. That's what a short conversation with my mother can do. After talking to her for two minutes you can feel like killing yourself.

Actually, I wasn't even sore with Louie Louie any more, partly because he was the kind of guy who would not only ogle your own mother right in front of you, but then look at you when you were sore at him with such a comical expression, like a dog that's just sat in its own dish or something, that you'd suddenly feel more inclined to slap him on the back and tell him what a great guy he was than punch him in the face. And also partly because what he'd said was probably the proper thing to have said under the circumstances, and instead of being sore at him I should've been grateful. I should have thanked him for being so goddam gallant.

'You know something,' he said, once we were out on the street, and although I was still feeling lousy, I was just beginning to feel less lousy. 'You really shouldn't be so mean to your mother.'

He was right, of course. I was a terrible son. I knew it.

'Why don't you mind your own goddam business,' I told him. I was really fired up again all of a sudden. 'Just because you've got the hots for her. Jesus Christ, Louie Louie, what'd you have to go and tell her she was a knockout for, anyway?'

Louie Louie regarded me with a very straight, serious face. He looked like he was about to deliver a lecture on personal hygiene or something. 'Because,' he said, 'she's a damned attractive woman, that's why. And besides,' he added, and his straight, serious face dissolved into a leery smirk, 'I've got the hots for her.'

'Louie Louie, you're lucky I don't knock your fat head off for you.'

'Oh yeah?' he said, beginning to horse around. He started to dance around a little bit, like he was in a boxing ring, just before the bell rings. Like he was limbering up before a big bout. He even did a little soft-shoe shuffle. 'C'mon then, Montanna. Give me your best shot! I'm ready for ya. I'll murder ya. One punch. One punch. That's all it'll take.' We horsed around for a while, bobbing and ducking, throwing pretend punches, until Louie Louie's face turned the colour of stewed rhubarb, the same as it did every time he overexerted himself, which usually took about thirty seconds of horsing around, and then we stopped. But I'd really cheered the hell up, just horsing around like that with old Louie Louie. I'd already just about forgotten how lousy I'd felt only two minutes before, and what a terrible son I was. I hadn't quite, but I almost had.

Once we'd quit horsing around, Louie Louie wiped his brow with his hand. It was really streaming. 'Gad*zooks!*' he said. 'It's *hot*! You could fry an egg right here on the sidewalk.'

'You could fry an egg right on your forehead,' I told him. You could have too, but he was right. It *was* hot, and it was only early yet. The papers were already calling it the hottest summer ever, just like the year before, and the year before that. But Louie Louie could work up a sweat walking to the bathroom anyway. He'd even been to doctors about it. Apparently he had overactive sweat glands or something.

He started kidding around again. 'I'm *mel*ting! I'm *mel*ting!' he said, like he was a giant ice-cream cone, or that witch from Oz.

'Louie Louie,' I told him, 'the amount you sweat, it's a wonder you're not a goddam puddle. You're like a walking sprinkler.' He opened his mouth to protest but I beat him to it. 'I know, I know,' I said. 'You've got overactive sweat glands.'

He grinned, wiping his brow some more. 'Well, I have,' he said, holding out his hand. 'Look. Real sweat.'

I'm really not too crazy about sweat. I know that's hardly unusual or anything, but I think I've got a bit of a phobia about it. Especially other people's. Louie Louie's is all right, because I'm so used to it. But anyone else's. Apart from being so lazy, that's probably the main reason I'm not too crazy about sport as well. It's hard to play sport and not sweat, unless it's something like archery or croquet maybe. As little kids it's not so bad because you can run around all day and not even do it. It's not so bad if you're playing outside, either, and if you don't get too close to anyone, but if it's inside, I really can't stand it. I especially can't stand places that smell of sweat all the time, like school gyms and locker rooms. Places like that just ooze old, stale, putrid sweat. You can smell just about every guy that's ever sweated in a place like that, which is very unpleasant. Personally, I don't know how people can spend much time in places like that. If I ever have to, which I avoid, I usually like to hold my breath, or for longer periods of time stuff tissues up my nose. People sometimes make smart comments, as you'd expect, but I couldn't give a damn.

Then, while Louie Louie was still catching his breath and sweating all over the sidewalk, a very unusual thing happened. Someone suddenly opened up their big trap and started singing at the top of their lungs. Just like that. They weren't singing along with anything either. They were just singing. They really had a terrific voice too, if you like that kind of thing. Personally, I wasn't a big opera fan. But when whoever it was that was singing hit a couple of particularly high notes I actually got the chills.

We looked around to see where it was coming from. Framed in a third-floor window right across the street we saw a woman the size of a battleship. She kind of reminded me of a battleship too, not just because she was built like one, but because of the way she was dressed. She was wearing armour and a horned helmet, and brandishing what looked like a trident, or possibly only a pitchfork. She was really belting it

56

out. I half expected thunderbolts to come crashing out of the sky.

'It's a goddam Viking!' said Louie Louie.

I didn't know what she was singing about (I think maybe it was in German) but I could tell she was mad as hell about something. Anyone could tell that much. She was making a louder noise than I thought it was possible for a human being to make only using their vocal cords. She was even drowning out the piped muzak and continuous flow of celebrity/war gossip that oozed out of the streetscreens all day long, which I guess might have been the point. That kind of thing can really get on people's nerves. Like the guy who once sat next to me on a bus and told me piped muzak was the slowest form of torture known to man. He didn't work up to it or anything, either. You know, by talking about the weather or something first, just to get acquainted. He just came right out with it, which I actually quite admire. I mean, if there's something you want to discuss, or get off your chest, I think it's a good idea just to do it. I don't see why you have to spend hours working the conversation round to what you actually want to talk about, or what's even worse, trying to find something that you both *want* to talk about. I think people when they're going to have a conversation should just come right out and say I'd like to talk about this, this or this. Give the other person a clear choice of topics, but make sure it's something you're interested in discussing in the first place. I think it would save a lot of time and pointless conversation. The thing is, though, in this case I really didn't have much to say on the subject, and besides, he hardly gave me time to say anything anyway. Once he'd finished telling me it was the slowest form of torture known to man, he just started laughing his head off all of a sudden, and wouldn't stop. He was still laughing a couple of blocks later when he got off.

But then, just when they were almost drowned out, all the nearby streetscreens started automatically getting louder. Maybe they were programmed to do it to combat increased background noise, like traffic and riots. But then, with an almost superhuman effort, the Viking started getting louder as well. You should have heard her. She was certainly giving her voice box quite a workout, but she was only flesh and blood. She couldn't keep it up for ever. It wasn't long before the strain started to show. First her face turned an alarming shade of purple, even darker than Louie Louie's does, and we could see her popping veins from clear across the road. Then steam started to hiss from her ears. Windows exploded all along the street.

'*Jesus Christ!*' Louie Louie shouted above the crazy, deafening din. 'I think she's gonna blow!'

Suddenly I couldn't stand it any more. My head was throbbing, my brain beating with a mad, insistent, booming pulse all its own, like an enormous drum keeping double, triple time. I felt my skull beginning to split open, from end to end, directly exposing my brain to the violently vibrating air. When I felt a trickle at my ear and put my hand up to feel it, it was wet.

I looked at the tips of my fingers and frowned.

'Look,' I said to Louie Louie. 'Real blood.'

But he couldn't hear me, his hands were clamped tight over his ears. Across the road the Viking suddenly exploded, spraying her room and the street below with great chunks of fatty raw flesh.

I thought I could hear them sizzle as they hit the ground.

18

To borrow a pretty corny line, everyone came to Moriarty's. At least, not everyone, but just about everyone I ever knew. It was a pretty nice place too. A bit run-down, maybe, but it definitely had character. The kind of place you could feel right at home. Old Moriarty, the proprietor (and a personal friend), was a good guy too, although people could get on his wrong side. He could be as sore as a bear with a ten-martini hangover at times. This was perfectly understandable, though, as he was a real-life incurable insomniac. Hadn't slept a wink in twenty-three years. Imagine that. He told me this himself one day, right out of the blue, and then just looking at his face you could tell it was true. I don't know why he told me. I guess maybe he just needed to tell *some*one, so he told me. He didn't say it was some big secret or anything, but I didn't tell anyone else all the same. Except Louie Louie, of course, and then what did he do but go and blab it to everyone in sight. I told you before he was a loudmouth. Now everyone knew. But Moriarty was fine about it. He didn't mind.

Another time he said, 'You know what I miss most about sleep?' I didn't. 'Waking up,' he said.

It was a very interesting observation, I thought. I mean, every morning when you wake up, theoretically at least, just about anything's possible. It really is. I mean, it isn't *actually* possible, but you kind of think it is.

It doesn't matter how crappy the day before might have been, or even that today's more than likely going to be just as crappy, or maybe even crappier. There's the possi-*bility* that things aren't going to be crappy, and that makes all the difference.

And something else that's kind of interesting, when you stop to think about, is just how many day-to-day expressions aren't even applicable to an insomniac in the first place. *Slept like a log. Got out of bed on the wrong side. Let's sleep on it. You'll feel better in the morning*, for example. It must have been rough on old Moriarty, what with people forever coming out with stuff like that. That's just the kind of thing that would really rub it in.

'Howzyashakes, boys?'

We were sitting up at the counter where we usually sat, except for when we sat in one of the booths. We were sitting on a couple of high stools which you could swing right round on if you felt like it, although Moriarty wasn't too crazy about people swinging round and round just for the hell of it, like it was a ride or something. He didn't mind Louie Louie and me doing it, though, not that we did it so much any more. He always asked us how our shakes were, and not just for the sake of it, either, like people do, but because he was genuinely interested. He wanted to know if they ever didn't come up to scratch. They always did, but even if they didn't, and you told him, he wouldn't have minded. He'd have thanked you. What he *would* have minded was someone criticising them behind his back. Anyway, I gave him one of my pet answers, as usual, which he always seemed to enjoy, acknowledging them with a soft chuckle, or on a bad day maybe a wan smile.

I said, 'If they were any better, Mr Moriarty, I couldn't stand it.'

Of course, old Moriarty never *expect*ed to be called Mister, but we both got a kick out of it, and to tell you the truth, he deserved the respect. A lot of people don't and that's all anyone ever calls them. Old Moriarty, apart from serving up just about the best milkshakes in the history of milkshakes, and providing a very welcoming environment for his patrons, was a real gentleman, even with his occasional tendency to take a swing at customers with a baseball bat. Not often or anything, I don't mean, just once in a while.

He was giving the counter in front of us the once-over with a cloth, the same as he probably did a thousand times a day. That was one of the things about Moriarty's. It was a bit run-down, but it was clean. It was just about the cleanest joint in town. I guess he had plenty of time to kill.

'So,' he said, leaning in towards us in a very conspiratorial way. 'What you boys up to today – *eh*?' He always asked like that, like he suspected – or at least hoped – we actually *were* up to something. Like maybe the overthrow of the government, perhaps. A goddam *coup* or something. Louie Louie thought he was probably a retired terrorist, or revolutionary maybe, and he could've been right. It wouldn't have surprised me a bit. He certainly looked like some kind of anarchist. But it wasn't the only wild rumour about him. There were so many, in fact, sometimes it was hard to keep up with them. Some people said he worshipped Satan and performed human sacrifices, for Chrissakes. Others said he had magic powers, and could stop time. And just about everyone, I guess, had heard about the enormous, labyrinthine library (or else a dungeon, where he kept the skeleton of his dead wife still shackled to a wall) under the premises. A person could get lost down there for days, so people said. I'd heard, too, that old Moriarty had read every book in the place, most of them twice. Even the rats, apparently, were well-read. Personally, I never saw him reading so much as a comic book, although he certainly knew some very unusual things for someone running a diner. In fact, people claimed he was just about every damn thing from double-jointed to undead, although perhaps the weirdest thing I ever heard was that not only did he have a third nipple, but a third, lidless eye smack bang in the middle of it.

Before answering his question, though, the one about what we were up to, Louie Louie glanced around, very furtively, like someone from some hilarious old spy movie where even the walls had ears. Then he leant forward and said, 'Not a single, solitary, goddam thing,' and gave old Moriarty a big, fat wink. 'And that's a fact.'

Moriarty tapped the side of his nose with a finger, before applying his cloth to an invisible speck of nearby dirt. He knew all about the rumours, of course, even the one about his dead, shackled wife.

'I tell you, boys,' he said, with a strange, faraway look in his eyes, 'these are the days of your lives.'

19

On the subject of sleep, I might just mention here that it's the one thing I'm any damn good at. I've always been good at it, ever since I was a little kid. Ever since I can remember. I've never been one of those guys who excel at every single thing they put their hand to, you know, without even seeming to try or anything. You know the kind I mean. If they can be bothered turning up, you just know they're going to be world champions at it. It doesn't matter whether it's splitting the atom or chewing gum. I've actually known one or two guys like that. They were nice guys, too, very friendly and personable, but everyone still hated their guts. You can't help hating a guy like that's guts. It's impossible. Even the friends of guys like that hate their guts. They just hide it better than everyone else.

No, sadly I was never one of those guys. I say 'sadly' because, to be honest with you, who the hell doesn't want to be a genius? The only person who could honestly tell you that they wouldn't want to be a genius would be a genius themself, and then it'd be a lie.

Don't get me wrong, though. I don't want to give you the wrong impression. I might not have been part of any think tanks or the captain of the lacrosse team exactly, but I wasn't completely hopeless. I wasn't a moron or anything, and at least people didn't actually groan when I got picked on their side or something, like they do with some kids. That kind of thing must be very disheartening. It can't do much for a kid's self-esteem. I try not to do it myself, even though I do anyway, sometimes. Not because I give a damn about who's on my team or anything, but just because it's an easy habit to fall into sometimes. With some kids when they're picked for a team it's kind of a preconditioned response. It's almost automatic. What I was, was average. I know it. I was average as hell, which isn't so bad. Except at sleeping, that is. I know it's not going to win me any medals or anything, but I can sleep just about anywhere, anytime. I really can. And I don't even have to be tired. If I'm in the right mood, I can sleep two or three days straight, just for the hell of it. I'll even wake up for meals, then go straight back to sleep again. At one time people even started calling me Coma Boy on account of my being able to fall into an instant deep sleep, in class or on the bus or wherever, and then being able to snap straight out of it again as soon as the bell rang or we arrived wherever it was we were going. But then another kid from school went into an *actual* coma, and it became a little confusing. What happened to the kid who went into an actual coma was an apple dropped on his head. That was it. Just like it did on old Isaac Newton's, except this particular apple didn't drop off a tree he was sitting under at the time, which would hardly have sent him into a coma if it had, but out of a clear blue sky. One minute he was just tripping along, apparently, chatting to some other kids, and the next – *pow!* – he was out cold. Still is. And then, not long after that, and I mean only a couple of *days* after, you'd have thought he'd been called Coma Boy all his life. That was all anyone was calling him. It wouldn't have surprised me if his own parents were calling him that.

At first people just assumed someone must've thrown the apple, or that it had been dropped out of a plane or something, but it hadn't been. I mean, it wasn't an isolated incident. Pretty soon fruit started falling all over the country, and not only apples. There were reports of oranges and nectarines and grapefruit and even pomegranates, which are as hard as they sound, as well as all kinds of other fruit that I can't remember now. Soon parents were too afraid to let their kids play in the park. Some parents wouldn't even let their kids walk to school unless they promised to follow extremely complicated routes specially worked out in advance so they'd be under cover the entire way. People were afraid to leave their houses, and if they did venture out they went about hugging the walls of buildings so closely they had to clamber over anyone else coming along the other way. That, or else they spent so much time looking up, ready to leap out of the way of plummeting fruit, they'd eventually walk under a bus or something. In fact, for a while there you could have been excused for thinking any open space was certain death. All we needed was for goddam watermelons to start falling out of the sky. They never did, though.

20

Sooner or later, just sitting there at the counter the way we were, Louie Louie's thoughts were guaranteed to return to food. They always did, sooner or later. He was always thinking about food or sex. One or the other. 'I think I might get something to eat,' he said. He announced it like it was some big news flash, like he was announcing a new battle front or something. He was always making announcements about very banal things. I don't know what he'd do if he ever had anything really important to announce. He'd have to organise a fanfare.

I probably should have been hungry, too, especially as I didn't have any breakfast, but I wasn't. All I'd had was a cup of coffee with four sugars in it and a milkshake, and I didn't even drink the coffee. I spilled most of it when I thumped the table. I can actually eat quite a lot when I'm in the mood, even though people generally think I must eat like a sparrow. They think that because I'm a little underweight for my height. I'm not skinny, but I'm definitely underweight. I've tried to put some on, but I just can't do it. I've got a very fast metabolism, apparently. People, when they see me eating a lot, when I'm in the mood, I mean, are always saying things like, 'Boy, you must have a really fast metabolism.' Sometimes they say it like having one was somehow cheating or something, like saying, 'Boy, you must have really good connections,' when someone gets into a good school or gets a good job. Then other people say it like it's a compliment, the same as they'd say, 'Boy, you really have a nice backhand,' to someone who was good at tennis. When girls say it, though, you can tell they just wish they had one too, even when they're already as thin as sticks. I can't take any credit for it, though. It's nothing to do with me.

'You know,' I said, 'you really should swallow one meal before you start another one. I'm not kidding. Otherwise they're likely to get all backed up and you'll need a plunger to force 'em down.'

'Better that than being nothing but a bag of bones,' said old Louie Louie. 'You must be terrified of dogs.'

'Who's a bag of bones? I'm wiry, is all.'

'You just about rattle when you walk. You'll make a beautiful skeleton at Halloween. You won't even need a costume.'

'No wonder, when you're always gorging yourself on my goddam breakfast. If I went near it I'd probably lose a hand.'

'Don't worry. I'd spit it out again. Too bony. Anyway, can I help it if I've got a healthy appetite?'

'Healthy?' I said. 'You make a swarm of locusts look like picky eaters. When you say you could eat a horse, you mean you could eat a horse.'

'Wuddaya expect? I'm a growing boy. I burn up a lot of energy.'

'Doing what exactly?'

'Eating, of course.'

Boy, you should have heard us. We amused the hell out of ourselves. We really did. We never got tired of horsing around like that, like some Howard Hawks movie or something, even though I know for a fact other people could find it very annoying. A couple of kids horsing around like that for too long can drive just about anybody nuts. Then Louie Louie ordered two hamburgers with the lot. I was still chuckling when I heard someone call my name.

'Hey, Montanna!'

I spun around on my seat to see who it was. I shouldn't have even bothered, though, because it was only old Baloney Maroney. That's what we should have called him: Only Old Baloney Maroney. I should probably point out that he was a real ray of sunshine. In fact, when I saw who it was, I just swung right back round to my milkshake again, and ignored the hell out of him.

But old Baloney Maroney could never take a hint, and pulled up a stool right next to me. He sat so close I could smell his socks, which wasn't difficult, as he hardly ever changed them.

'Hey, Montanna,' he said again, and I could tell, just by the way he said it, that he had something on his mind.

But I just ignored the hell out of him some more. I was pretty sure I knew what he was working up to anyway, so there was no point encouraging him. Whatever he had to say, he'd say it, whether I was interested in hearing it or not. In fact, old Baloney Maroney, in all the time I'd known him, had never said anything to anyone that they'd particularly wanted to hear. He was just one of those very miserable guys who go about with their own personal little black cloud trailing after them, waiting to rain on everybody else's parade. The only way he could make himself feel good, I guess, was by making someone else feel bad.

'I heard you stepped off the kerb into the path of a goddam speeding car,' he said at last, I guess when he realised he was being ignored for sure. I'm surprised it took him so long. He should have been used to it. 'What are you?' Here he paused for about ten seconds for effect. He'd probably rehearsed it and everything. 'Some kind of *re*tard or something?' He said it like it was just the wittiest crack imaginable, like he was Noël Coward or somebody, and looked around to see who might have heard him say it. He looked like he was expecting a round of applause. Or people to come up and congratulate him. I don't mind admitting it, he could really irritate a person if they gave him half a chance.

However, what I did was, I didn't say anything for about a full minute. I just sat there, almost like I hadn't even heard him, casually drinking my milkshake. I could feel old Baloney Maroney just sitting there next to me smirking his stupid head off, though, like he'd just scored a terrific victory. He was a terrible smirker. He could have smirked professionally if there'd been anyone interested in paying him to do it. Then what I did was I just turned round and said, like I was commenting on the weather or something, 'Hey, Baloney Maroney, why don't you ever change your socks? Boy, they really stink.'

Whatever he'd been expecting me to say, it wasn't that. It definitely took him by surprise.

'*Huh?*' he said.

'Your socks. They stink. It smells like you've got gangrene of the feet or something. If I were you, I'd see a doctor,' I told him, '*asagp.*'

For a second there, old Baloney Maroney must've thought I was serious. To be honest, he wasn't too bright. He was actually a pretty dumb kid. Mean and dumb, which is just a terrific combination. He looked so comical, suddenly, all concerned about his possibly gangrenous feet, that Louie Louie and I just burst out laughing. I would've liked to string him along a bit longer, but I couldn't do it.

'Too bad you didn't break your stinking neck, Montanna!' he said. He really spat the words out. I told you he was mean. He looked like he'd quite happily break it for me himself. He'd enjoy it. Then he flounced the hell out.

It was quite hilarious, but I could still smell his socks.

21

Once Louie Louie had finished polishing off his couple of hamburgers with the lot, which took about sixty seconds flat, and we'd both had another milkshake, we thought about playing the pinball machines, which we used to be crazy about, but in the end we couldn't be bothered. Sometimes for something to do we took turns playing them with our eyes closed, and whoever didn't have them closed would have to tell the other one when to shoot. Or we'd play them backwards, facing the wrong way. It was pretty stupid and a waste of time but we did it anyway. But today we couldn't even be bothered doing that. We also thought about just mooching about where we were, but in the end we decided to take off instead, even though we didn't have anywhere particular to go. But I liked it that way. I preferred it. If I had more than two things I had to do in a day it'd exhaust me. So then we bade old Moriarty so long.

'So long, boys,' he said back, flicking us a weary half salute. Poor bastard. I just bet he wouldn't have minded tagging along with us. Maybe I should have invited him. 'And whatever you do, remember – don't get caught.'

After being inside for so long, it was bright as hell out on the street. There wasn't a cloud in the crummy sky. There probably wasn't a cloud for a thousand miles. White light dazzled our eyes and the sidewalk felt hot and hard under my feet. It felt hot and hard and unyielding, like it was concrete all the way down. Cities sometimes feel like that. Like they're concrete all the way down. Sometimes they feel like they're not even part of the planet at all. It's like they're their own planet, made of metal and concrete and glass, and everyone living in them, or on them, is an alien or something, not human at all. Sometimes I felt like that, too. Other times I felt everyone else was like that. Not even human. Big deal, I guess. Anyway, it was bright as hell. The sky looked like it was made of shiny sheet metal. Hot and hard and bright as steel. It looked like you could sharpen an axe on it. Any second now Louie Louie would be sweating buckets again. Beads of perspiration were already breaking out on his top lip and huddling beneath his floppy fringe.

He pushed it back. 'Ice . . .' he said, and left the word dangling in the air.

'Box!' I said, right on cue, before it had time to melt. 'Ice . . .'

'Berg! Ice . . .'

'Land! Ice . . .'

'Scream!'

'You . . .'

'Scream!'

'We all . . .'

'Scream!'

'*Aaaaaaaaaaaaaahhhhhhhh!*'

We must have done that a million times since we first thought of it. We hadn't done it in a while, though. We used to do it all the time once, when we were kids. It nearly used to kill us. I don't even know when we stopped. I don't know what made Louie Louie think of

73

it then, but I was glad he did. It didn't kill us any more, but we both got a terrific bang out of it all the same, and felt like little kids again. Then we kind of just looked around, maybe for some inspiration or whatever. But instead everything just seemed to be moving in slow motion somehow, and not only that, but slightly out of sync as well, including Louie Louie and me. The day felt like it was wrapped in great thick blankets of heat. It was really stifling. I suddenly felt about as lethargic as a corpse, like I didn't have enough energy to tie my own shoelace. If you'd asked me what time it was I couldn't have been bothered even telling you. I couldn't have told you anyway, because I almost never wear a watch, but I couldn't have been bothered anyway. Maybe if we'd had the energy we might have turned around and gone back inside again and had another milkshake, but we didn't. So instead, with nothing else to do and nowhere to go, what we did was we just allowed ourselves to drift along, heading nowhere and in no particular hurry to get there, as if we were riding some gently rolling wave, but not one that was ever going to break someplace. It felt like it might just keep on rolling for ever, maybe, to the ends of the earth even, wherever that might be. That's what it felt like.

The streets were quite empty for the time of day, and the people we did pass seemed to be drifting by us in a trance, like people who are busy thinking about this or that, or nothing maybe, and have given their bodies over to whatever force it is that keeps people putting one foot in front of the other. Even the traffic was gliding by as if the cars were all on cruise control and their drivers asleep at the wheel, except for one woman who looked exactly like Audrey Hepburn in an open-top sports car who might or might not have smiled at me as she passed by.

No one paid any attention to the bombed-out buildings with their giant billboards hiding the rubble, telling us to TRUST and SPEND, and the occasional one reminding us where we were, that just said AMERICA. One hole in the ground was a lot like another, I guess, and we were used to holes in the ground (though once I thought I saw a giant rabbit disappear down one, but I might have been mistaken). We didn't talk either, we just kept on rolling, like we were part of some enormous, invisible body of water, slow-moving and directionless, flowing with the tide. But of course everything has a direction, even if it doesn't know it. You can't take two goddam steps without one. You think you can, but you can't. And I guess that was how we finally found ourselves washed up on the stinking old beach, miles out of town, amidst all the filth and stench, without even meaning to. If you'd asked me how we'd got there, I might have said walked, but I'd have been only guessing.

Old Louie Louie looked around, almost in surprise, like we'd been teleported there or something. Or like we'd been sleepwalking. I guess I did the same. I could feel the sand grinding under my feet. It felt like glass.

'Goddam beach,' he said.

'Looks like it,' I said.

22

What a dump. I couldn't believe it, it was so crummy. It was just about the crummiest place you can imagine. It was worse even than I remembered. The beach sure isn't what it once was, even if you can't believe the movies. All those old beach movies made a thousand years ago, I mean, when all anyone ever did was go surfing and build bonfires and then sit around them playing corny old songs on guitars. If you ask me, that kind of thing looked pretty repetitious, to be honest, but I guess it might have been fun all the same. If you were actually *there*, I mean, with old Moondoggy and Jughead or whoever. If you were there with *those* guys. You wouldn't be able to do it now, though. You'd never get away with it. Everyone would be much too cynical to just sit around a bonfire singing nowadays. You'd be laughed out of town if you tried that now. You wouldn't last two minutes. But back then it might have been fun. You never know. But watching those movies now's like watching life on an entirely different planet. I mean, could people have ever really lived like that? Kids and teenagers, I mean. It doesn't seem very likely, but who the hell knows. And maybe they even still *do*, *some*where. Maybe somewhere there's a regular beach blanket bingo still going on, with Moondoggy and Jughead and all those cute girls in polka-dot bikinis. If there is, I'm glad, and if not, well I still get a bang out of watching them all the same, sometimes. And there's still something about a polka-dot bikini and a beach ball that makes me all nostalgic, even though I've never been near either one in my life.

And that's another thing. I don't know what it is, but I must have spent half my life feeling nostalgic about one damn thing or another. It just comes natural to me, like sleeping and staring at the ceiling. I think someone or other famous once called it a disease. I can't remember who it was, but he was right. It's not as bad as a lot of other diseases, obviously, but that's what it is.

Take the war, for example. Not this one, or the last one, or any of the others I don't mean. I mean WWII, back when they had a beginning *and* an end, and some-times even a middle. I know it must have been quite a crummy time to be around and all, but I still can't help feeling all nostalgic about it, as if I'd actually been there or something. It's strange. I don't even know if people who were actually there ever felt nostalgic about it, but *I* did. But it's not really the war itself, of course. I've never felt particularly nostalgic about getting shot, or blown up, or tortured by the Gestapo or anything. It's the *at*mosphere that gets me. The movies and the music and all the camaraderie. Take the Blitz, for example. Although it must have been pretty lousy and everything, what with people getting blown to bits in their own beds, and having to watch television in their gas masks, it seemed to bring out the best in people. Like in that old movie, *Mrs Miniver*, which I must have seen about fifty times at least. I'm crazy about that movie. That final scene in the bombed-out old church, with the sun rays bursting through the smashed roof at the end, just kills me every time. Also when the husband, Walter Pidgeon, goes off in his little motorboat to rescue trapped Tommies at Dunkirk. I can't imagine people doing that today. No way. They'd be too afraid of getting their boat scratched. They'd be worried about whether their insurance covered getting goddam strafed or not. And apart from that, everybody'd be too terrified anyway. Everybody'd be screaming, 'Don't we *pay* people to do that stuff?' and peeing their pants at the thought of having to do it themselves. And another thing. I know it's hard to believe, but they even had *sing*alongs. Imagine that! Complete strangers crammed into the subway like sardines, all singing their heads off to keep their spirits up, while up above them their homes and lives were being blown all to hell. But then, sometimes, I actually feel kind of bad about it. About feeling so nostalgic, I mean. After all, I realise it must have been really terrible in reality, with a lot of very crummy stuff going on. I guess I sometimes just feel kind of guilty for feeling so nostalgic about it all, especially when I wasn't even born. Like I'm not entitled. But then I can just as easily feel the same way about something that happened only last week. And the thing is, it doesn't even have to be anything important, or even memorable. I can feel nostalgic about even very boring things. It just has to be over. Some disease.

But as I was saying, a day at the beach sure isn't what it was. No kidding. Not a polka-dot bikini or beach ball in sight. It was like a deserted island, although it was more like a garbage dump. Not even a Robinson Crusoe and his Man Friday, unless of course they were us, Louie Louie and me. This was hardly surprising, though. People don't go to the beach any more. For one thing, it's too hot, and for another, the sea's a swamp. No, not even a swamp. What it is is sludge. Beautiful, black, stinking sludge. It doesn't move, doesn't ebb, doesn't flow, doesn't do a damn thing. It's dead, and everything in it is dead. Except maybe it can still dream, kind of just sit there and dream about better days and polka-dot bikinis, maybe. Least I hope so.

It was kind of strange how we'd ended up there, without really intending to or anything, but now that we were there I guess we thought we might as well stick around. We thought we'd sit and watch the sludge for a while, so we found a suitable spot amongst all the refuse, the piles of rotting tyres, abandoned wrecks and rusting air conditioners. The mountains of stinking garbage were home to rats, real giants, who just ignored the hell out of us. They could afford to. They must have outnumbered us a million to one. And although it smelled pretty awful, we made ourselves comfortable all the same, just sitting there gazing at that lovely sludge. And the sludge just sat there, too, glistening quietly in the sun. It really glistened. It even gleamed. In a way it was pretty goddam beautiful.

'Boy,' said Louie Louie at last, 'beach culture sure the hell ain't what it used to be.' He was sitting there, squinting out to sea, and I just knew he was thinking of all those girls in polka-dot bikinis. I told you before. He was sex mad.

'Guess not,' I said.

I picked up a stone that was just lying there and tossed it at the water. It skimmed across the top, four or five times, then stopped and slowly sank.

'Hey, Louie Louie,' I said, suddenly thinking about something else. 'Do you really think my mother's a knockout, or did you just say it – you know – to make her feel better?' I don't even know why I wanted to know. I just thought I'd ask.

He looked kind of surprised at the question, like maybe he'd never even thought about it before. He probably hadn't, either. He wasn't generally very introspective. Then he looked as though he'd thought of something to say, but just as quickly decided not to say it. Knowing Louie Louie, it was probably something very tasteless and crude. Usually he'd have said it, too. He was always saying stuff like that.

'Hell, Montanna,' he said instead, '*I* dunno.'

The sludge had swallowed the stone so completely by now, without leaving so much as a ripple, that I might never have tossed it. Then I thought, thanks to me, that stone would never, in the history of the world, see the light of day again. The shiny black surface had closed over it like a vault. It might never even have existed.

'Hey, Louie Louie,' I said again, thinking about the stone, and the sludge, and maybe even old Moondoggy and Jugears, 'do you ever wonder how things'll turn out?'

He was still staring at the sludge, although it was

harder to tell what he was thinking about now. If he wasn't thinking about food or sex, it was quite difficult to guess.

Then he said, 'Howdja mean, exactly – "turn out"?'

'You know,' I said. 'In the end?'

23

What I meant, I guess, was when we were old. Not just older, but old. It was something I thought about, sometimes. I don't know why. I guess everyone thinks about stuff like that every now and then. It's only natural. The thing is, though, I thought about it quite a lot. Not in a morbid way or anything, although I sometimes thought about it in that way as well. You know, about not being able to use the bathroom by myself, for example, or having to be fed with a goddam spoon. I really wasn't looking forward to that. When I did think about being old in a morbid kind of way, and I thought about things like not even being able to use the bathroom or being fed with a spoon, I'd tell myself that before I got to that stage I'd just end it. I'd kill myself. I even knew how I'd do it.

I could never shoot myself or hang myself or anything like that. My main problem with things like shooting yourself or hanging yourself is that someone always has to find you, afterwards, which really can't be very pleasant for them. No one wants to find their loved one or even a complete stranger with the back of their head blown off or dangling from the ceiling with their tongue hanging out. People have enough to deal with without that. And even when you take an overdose, someone still has to find you and clean you up and stuff. In fact, almost every way you look at it, there are quite serious obstacles to killing yourself in such a way as not to cause any unnecessary inconvenience or unpleasantness to others. There really are. Which is where my idea comes in.

It would take a little preparation and planning, of course, but it'd be worth it. Basically, what I'd do is I'd go to some quite remote area. The desert would probably be best, plus I've always particularly liked the desert, although I've never actually been to one. Then I'd set up a few things that I would have taken with me, like a comfortable armchair and a small table and a thermos of tea and probably a book. There might also be one or two other things that I was very attached to, and maybe a framed photograph or two placed on the table. I might even have some music playing in the background, but nothing depressing or anything like that. Nothing too ponderous. Some Gershwin might be nice, but nothing too big-band. Nothing too brassy. And then around this in a circle I'd scatter a whole bunch of kindling, and then drench it in some kind of odourless but highly flammable fuel. Not petrol or kerosene because of the smell. And then, somehow or other, I'd set up some kind of mechanism for setting off a chain reaction which would result in the kindling being set alight. I'd probably do this by attaching a piece of string to my toe, which, when I twitched it, would activate the mechanism. This part needed some fine-tuning, I admit, but it wouldn't be a problem. And finally, before I set the whole thing off, I'd take a whole bottle of sleeping pills and then just sit back drinking my tea and reading my book or maybe just enjoying the desert air. As I said, I've never been to the desert, but I'm pretty sure I'd enjoy the air there. I've heard it's very nice. And then, sooner or later, I'd just pass out, my toe would give a twitch, the mechanism for setting the kindling alight would be activated and – *whoosh!* – the whole thing would go up in flames. Simple. With me sitting right in the middle of it, happily dreaming away of beach balls and cute girls in polka-dot bikinis, maybe.

Of course, I didn't think about this all the time. About being so old I couldn't even go to the bathroom by myself, or else going up in flames out in the desert. Overall, I actually thought it might be fun. Being old, I mean. I was kind of looking forward to it, to tell you the truth. Most old people I ever saw either went about being old like it was a mild inconvenience or else like it was a real pain in the side. But occasionally, just occasionally, I'd see some old guy or old lady who went about as if they were having a ball. Like they thought being old was a real blast. You could tell just by looking at them that they were thoroughly enjoying themselves. It was rare, I admit, but you still saw it every now and then. It gave me a real blast myself to see someone like that. It really did.

I remember one old guy in particular. I was in the park this day, just strolling along, minding my own business, when I saw him. He was this very old guy just ahead of me. I could've overtaken him quite easily, but for some reason I kind of liked the look of him, and was happy just to stroll along behind him. For one thing he was very well dressed, but not in an exaggerated way. He wasn't fashionable or anything. Old people should never dress fashionably, if you ask me. It doesn't suit them. In fact, this guy was dressed kind of *old*-fashioned, and looked a little worn around the edges as well, but elegant, too. I couldn't see his face but I really liked the look of him, and was sure that when I *did* see it, I'd like it too. Anyway, what happened was that after strolling around for a while, he suddenly started towards this big old tree standing all by itself. I don't know what kind of tree it was because I'm quite ignorant about nature, but it was some tree, that's for sure. It was autumn, and the park looked like it was on fire or something. It was very picturesque. This particular tree looked like an enormous flaming torch. It was really something. Anyway, what he did was, this old guy, who by the look of him must have been about a hundred, once he'd got to the tree he started to clamber up it. I couldn't believe it. He was pretty agile, too, considering. The bottom branch was quite low to the ground, luckily, and he managed to get hold of it reasonably easily and then he half swung, half dragged himself up onto it. Then from there he positively scooted up it. I was pretty surprised, that's for sure. I really hadn't been expecting him to do anything like that. He was this incredibly ancient old guy, and there he was scooting up a tree like a squirrel, in broad daylight, too. Admittedly it was nice weather for that kind of thing, but I didn't see anyone else doing it all the same, not even any little kids. Kids don't so much any more, I find. No one does. But the funny thing is, seeing that old guy do it suddenly made *me* feel like doing it. I felt suddenly guilty about *not* climbing trees. I thought, if he can be bothered doing it, at his age, if he can be bothered making the effort, then what's stopping me? But then I thought, not unnaturally, well of course he's out climbing trees because he's demented.

He must be. But *then* I thought, well, better out climbing trees than shuffling about in some crummy old nursing home in carpet slippers trying to remember where he'd put his cup of crummy, tepid old nursing-home tea. If it was me, I'd rather be out climbing trees, too, even if it *did* mean I was demented.

Then I lost sight of him about halfway up as the leaves were too thick to see. I could still follow his progress, though, because I could see the leaves shaking all over the place as he made his way up higher and higher. It looked like the tree was having an epileptic fit or something. It was quivering all over. Before too long there was a pile of leaves a foot deep lying on the ground underneath. It was funny how even though the odd leaf was falling from the other trees they were raining down from just that one tree. It looked like the seasons were suddenly speeded up. Pretty soon it'd be snowing. Eventually, though, after not being able to see him for a little while, he suddenly reappeared at the very top. His head just popped up through the branches and leaves, like someone surfacing after swimming a long time underwater. And then, maybe for just a couple of seconds, a very strange thing happened. You might not believe it, but for a couple of seconds I could see and feel everything he could. It felt like I was looking out through his old-man eyes, and through them, just for that very short time, I was looking at a world that seemed to have suddenly clicked into perfect focus. I hadn't even realised it was *out* of focus, but it was. It had been out of focus the whole time and I never even knew it.

Somehow or other he'd managed to balance himself up amongst the uppermost branches, with not only his head but most of his body now visible. He must have been very precariously balanced, but still managed to look as reasonably steady as a terrifically old guy up a tree could be expected to look. He was still holding on, but then, rather optimistically, he let go all of a sudden. He wobbled for a moment, then regained his balance. Then he cupped both hands around his mouth and raised his face up to the sky. It looked like it had just been slapped on like a fresh coat of bright blue paint. Then he called out just about the last thing I expected a hundred-year-old guy up a tree to call out.

He said, 'KISS – MY – *ASS*!'

But almost immediately there was a tremendously loud *crack!* and he disappeared from sight. It actually looked very comical, to be honest, as if someone hiding below in the foliage had suddenly yanked him by the ankles. The tree just seemed to swallow him up, and then almost as quickly it spat him out again the other end.

I thought he'd be dead for sure, but by the time I reached him, not only was he not dead, he was smiling.

'*Jee*zus Christ!' I said. 'Are you okay, mister?' I was amazed he wasn't dead. He must have been a tough old bird.

He looked up at me from where he was lying on his back in a pile of old dead leaves. He had a very gentle smile on his crinkly old face, which I'd been right about, by the way – I *did* like the look of it. It was a good face. Then he started to giggle. He really looked as happy as a clam. Of course, I didn't know what to do. I thought I should probably call an ambulance or something, but I didn't want to leave him by himself.

'Somebody call a goddam ambulance!' I yelled, but

when I looked around, the park was deserted. Not even a goddam dog.

Meanwhile, the crazy old guy was still chuckling away quietly to himself. Something or other was really tickling his fancy. I couldn't imagine what it could be, though. It really wasn't a very humorous situation.

'Hey,' I said, partly to kind of humour him, I guess, and partly because I didn't know what else to say, 'what's so goddam funny?'

He looked at me for a second or two, like maybe he couldn't believe I didn't get it, then he burst right out laughing. He thought my question was hilarious. He'd only been giggling before, but now he laughed so hard he damn near choked. He even managed to cough up a little blood, which really scared the hell out of me.

'Take it easy, fella,' I told him, as soothingly as I could. I was shaking all over, I was so scared. 'Take it easy, hey.' But he just beckoned me closer with a tiny flutter of one hand.

I was already kneeling right down beside him amongst all those dead leaves. They crackled like tiny breaking bones beneath me as I leant in even closer. That close, I could see every line and wrinkle on his face. His whole face was a mass of them. He was the most ancient guy I'd ever seen. He was pretty repulsive, too, to be honest, although I know that sounds bad, and I don't really mean it anyway. I do, but I don't, if you know what I mean. He had a good face, and I really liked it and everything, but it was so old. And then I suddenly wondered whether he might have had a wife somewhere or other, and if so, whether she was as old and repulsive as he was. What a gorgeous couple, I thought.

I couldn't help it. But then the more I looked at him, the more I began to change my mind. I actually began to think he wasn't repulsive at all. I mean, the closer you looked at him you could tell that he'd probably been quite a handsome guy in his time, although that's not what I mean exactly. What I mean is, even now, once you got past the initial shock of it, especially up that close, you realised that what you at first thought was repulsive was actually beautiful. It was like a work of art or something. His face was so old and battered and lined and interesting it was like looking at a really terrific view. It was a face really worth looking at, if you could be bothered. But then I noticed his terribly laboured breathing, which scared me even more than the blood he'd coughed up.

He gave me a very weak, kind of reassuring smile, as if to say, 'Don't worry, kid, I'll be fine,' but it didn't work. It was a nice smile and everything, and I appreciated it, but I still had a very strong suspicion he was about to peg out any minute. He looked like he was going to say something, too, so I leant in even closer, straining to catch it. I didn't want to miss his last words or anything, in case someone asked me later what they were.

'It . . .'

He said it very softly, as weak as hell now. I waited patiently for the next word.

'was always . . .'

'Yes?' I encouraged him.

'going . . .'

'Ye-es?'

'to have . . .'

'*Uh huh?*'

'a happy . . .'

Come on, I thought, you crazy old bastard. You can do it. You're nearly there. Spit it out.

'ending.'

What?

I didn't understand.

What?

I sat back on my heels, staring at him. '*What* was always going to have a happy ending?' I asked him. Maybe I'd missed something. I really wanted to know, though. I was suddenly curious as hell. But then he just looked at me, and frowned.

'Hey,' he said, and his voice was suddenly stronger. He sounded much better. Maybe he wasn't going to cash his chips in after all. 'Don't I know you, kid?'

And then he died.

Back at the beach, Louie Louie was still thinking about it. About whether he ever thought about how things would turn out in the end. He thought about it so long I was just beginning to think he'd *stopped* thinking about it. He'd done that before, plenty of times. I'd ask him something and then I'd be standing there waiting for him to answer, thinking he was still thinking it over, because he *looked* as if he was thinking it over, and all the while he'd be busy thinking about something else entirely, like what he was going to have for lunch, for example. He'd have even forgotten I'd asked him anything. That's how he looked now, too, like he was considering it from every angle, but it was hard to tell, as I say. I didn't rush him, though, just in case.

Then he said, 'Nope. Guess not.'

I never told old Louie Louie about the old guy falling

out of the tree. I don't know why I never did, but I didn't. It's just the kind of thing you would tell someone, I know, but I never did. I thought about telling him plenty of times. I thought about telling him then, too, sitting on the beach, watching the sludge lapping at the filthy shore. I didn't, though. I never did.

24

I'd forgotten about the pier. I hadn't seen it since I was a kid. It had been derelict even back then, but it was worse now. It must have been pretty impressive once, though, years ago. In a way it still was. I'd seen old pictures of it, back in its heyday, when it was all shiny and new and lit up like a Christmas tree at night. It was quite something. It must have been nice to promenade up and down it on a hot summer's day, back then, eating ice cream and tipping your hat to passers-by. Or else going for a stroll of an early evening, with just the hint of a cool breeze coming up over the sea . . . (See what I mean? Goddam nostalgia again. I just can't help it.) But now, with all its paint peeling off in great flaky scales, it reminded me of a giant snake shedding its skin. And not just its skin, but its flesh as well. Its rotting timbers showed through like bleached ribs. And from a distance, I almost thought I could see it wriggling and writhing, like it was still alive, trying to shake itself free. Its skin was coming off in enormous flakes, and there was nothing beneath it but brittle old sun-bleached bones, a skeletal frame. Its insides had already been eaten away. Maybe I was being a bit fanciful, but the thing is, it did look a bit like a giant snake, just lying there basking and rotting in the sun.

'Hey, Louie Louie,' I said, on a sudden whim, not because I particularly wanted to or anything, but just for something to say, 'how about we investigate the old pier? Wuddaya say? Snoop around a bit. We could be the goddam Hardy Boys or something.'

Louie Louie turned around and looked at me less than enthusiastically, like I'd suggested walking up twenty-five flights of stairs. I wasn't exactly the most enthusiastic person in the world, as a rule, but Louie Louie made me look like a fanatic. I guess he was pretty comfortable where he was, thanks very much, even surrounded as we were by all that stinking garbage (in the heat you could actually see the stink coming off it). Besides, it didn't exactly look safe. The pier. In fact, the whole structure looked about as rickety as hell, like all it would take was a half-decent gust of wind and the whole thing would collapse. There was even an old security fence round the entrance to keep people out, I guess for their own safety. Not that I saw anyone clambering to get in or anything. And half the pylons supporting it had already rotted away. Actually, I was surprised any of them were still standing, considering what they were standing in. Of course, it was only a matter of time before the rest rotted away as well, and the whole thing just up and fell into the sea. I wondered if it'd disappear below the surface as completely as the rock I'd just thrown when it finally did.

Even though Louie Louie wasn't exactly brimming over with enthusiasm about the idea, now that I'd suggested it, I was actually quite excited about taking a look. It looked like it might be quite interesting, or at least more interesting than sitting there surrounded by garbage. 'Well, we can't just sit here all day,' I pointed out, although there wasn't really any reason why we couldn't. We didn't have anyplace else to rush off to all of a sudden. 'You know, just staring at the sea. Someone might come along and mistake you for a beached whale. They might think you're some kind of mutant whaleboy or something. Hell, they might even try and refloat you.'

'More like they'd mistake you for a lovesick *mer*man, pining for his mermaid,' Louie Louie shot back, quick as ink.

I loved that. Lovesick *mer*man!

'Oh yeah, blubber boy?'

'That's right, fish dick!'

'Well, take *that*!' I said, gutting him with a harpoon. 'And *that*, and *that*!'

Louie Louie writhed around on the sand, pretending to gush buckets of blood, before suddenly going all limp. Then, with his last dying breath, declared triumphantly, 'But little did the evil harpoonist suspect – toxic *blood*!'

'Ahhhhhhhhhhhhh!' I cried, contorting in agony, all covered in the stuff. 'I'm *mel*ting! I'm *mel*ting!'

We both collapsed, Louie Louie from his multiple harpoon wounds and me from being covered from head to toe in his toxic, flesh-eating blood, and just lay there, not moving a muscle, except for maybe an occasional death twitch. I could smell the rotting garbage and feel the sun like two heavy coins pressing against my eyelids.

'Last one to the fence sucks eggs!' cried Louie Louie, leaping to his feet.

25

The old wire fence was topped by nasty-looking coils of rusty barbed wire, with odd strands of faded old material caught up in it, flapping in the breeze like tiny ragged flags. An old metal sign was hanging on the locked gates, with TRESPASSERS WILL BE PROSECUTED written on it in faded paint. It really wasn't a very welcoming place, up close, that's for sure. Louie Louie, who could be quite creative when he felt like it, took out a coin and scratched a few adjustments on the sign. A minute later it said TRESPASSERS R CUTE instead. We didn't generally go about defacing public property, and he probably shouldn't have done it, but we both got a kick out of it all the same. Also, it wasn't like it was offensive or anything, which is something I find quite irritating. People scrawling stuff all over the place that's offensive just for the sake of it. I mean, TRESPASSERS R CUTE might be pretty dumb, I'll admit, but it's kind of clever as well. I think a lot of stuff you see scrawled all over the place shows a definite lack of imagination.

When Louie Louie had finished, he pushed at the gates to see how much they'd give. They were held together with a length of chain and a rusty padlock. If he thought he was going to squeeze through them, he was crazy. I couldn't even have done it. There was only about a six-inch gap.

'Too bad,' he said.

'Wuddaya goddam mean,' I asked him: 'too bad?'

'Goddam locked,' he said.

''Course it's locked. Naturally it's locked. They don't want people just strolling in any old time they feel like it, do they? That's what they put up this crazy old barbed-wire fence for. And the sign.' Louie Louie giggled when I said that. 'To keep people out.'

'That's what I goddam mean,' he said. 'Too bad.'

'You can climb, can't ya?' I asked him.

''Course I can climb,' he said. 'Like a cat.'

'Well, then?'

'Well then what?'

'Well then last one over's a big fat bastard!'

We both leapt up onto the fence like a couple of escapee convicts, and started clambering the hell up. I managed to negotiate the barbed wire at the top without too much difficulty, and jumped down the other side. Of course, Louie Louie got stuck. The fence was actually quite high, and he was in a rather precarious position, perched up there snagged on the barbed wire like that, but it was still an amusing situation. It was even more precarious and amusing because the fence wasn't terribly steady, and was starting to wobble about quite a bit. Every time Louie Louie moved it wobbled some more.

'So, who's a big fat bastard?' I called up to him. I was being very mature about it.

He hollered back at me, clinging on with white knuckles.

'Ya goddam sonuva*bitch*! I'm goddam *stuck*, for Chrissakes!'

'Boy, oh boy!' I said. I was really enjoying myself. I didn't want to rush it. I was standing on the ground looking up at him very leisurely with my hands on my hips like a real bastard. 'You look just like one of those old blimps that's bust its moorings and got caught up amongst the chimney pots.' This was actually something I'd seen on television once. It was from the Blitz, when there was a whole bunch of these blimps or whatever they were tied up above the city to stop planes coming in low and bombing the hell out of people. Anyway, one day one of them got loose, which caused quite a lot of damage (mostly to chimney pots), but was probably a nice distraction from getting the hell bombed out of you all the same. It probably took people's minds off it.

I wasn't by nature a cruel or sadistic person, not really, but it was such a golden opportunity to pay old Louie Louie back I couldn't resist it. Opportunities this good didn't come along every day. Also, he hadn't exactly been a prince when it came to divulging certain facts about a certain somebody. In fact, he'd really made me sweat. He'd extracted maximum enjoyment and it was only fair I got some back.

'I thought you said you could climb like a goddam wuddayacallit – a cat?' I asked him. 'I distinctly remember you saying you could climb like a cat.'

'Montanna, you lousy sonuvabitch! I'm getting dizzy up here!' He was really wailing away by this time, poor bastard. I was being a real louse. 'I think I'm gonna faint!'

I helped him down after that. Apart from anything else, he probably was going to faint. He'd done it before. It'd be Louie Louie all over to faint on top of a barbed-wire fence. Then I'd never have got him down. He left another ragged little flag up there, too, flapping with the others.

'Goddam it,' he said, back on solid ground again, and twisting round to take a look at the rip in his pants. 'I've scratched my ass!'

'Well, no one else was gonna scratch it for you,' I said.

He glared at me. 'For your information, this is exactly how people get lockjaw. I've read all about it. I could get lockjaw here and it'd be all your fault. Goddam *lock*jaw, for Chrissake!'

No one could be misinformed quite like Louie Louie. And once he'd got something into his head, no matter how far-fetched it might be, it was just about impossible to get it out again. One time, he even managed to convince himself that dolphins weren't really mammals because they didn't have external ear lobes. External ear lobes! It was the craziest thing I'd ever heard, but Louie Louie was convinced it was true because he'd read it somewhere or other, or thought he had. He believed all kinds of crazy stuff, most of it quite trivial but crazy all the same. He thought he was very reliably informed, too. He thought if you'd read something somewhere then it must be true. People do that all the time. They're nuts, though.

'You're not going to get lockjaw,' I told him. 'You can only get lockjaw if you're bitten by a rabid dog. Or a bat. All you've got is a teensy little scratch on your ass.'

Actually, I wasn't entirely sure *how* you got lockjaw, but I didn't see the point in admitting that to Louie Louie. It'd only encourage him. I mean, just let him get the idea that he *could* get lockjaw, and that'd be that. He'd be foaming at the mouth in two seconds flat.

'You *can* get it by being bitten by a rabid dog,' he agreed. 'That's true. *Or* a bat. You can even get it by being bitten by a ra*coon*. But it's a well-known and established fact that the majority of cases of lockjaw are caused by minor scratches from such things as barbed wire or old rusty cans.'

Louie Louie could embellish like a sonuvabitch. He really could. And the thing is, he thought every word was true. Even if he'd only just invented it himself. To listen to him, you'd think he'd written a goddam treatise on the subject or something.

'All right, ol' Yeller,' I told him. 'Just take it easy, old fella.'

Old Yeller, if you don't already know, was quite a famous film about a faithful old dog that gets lockjaw and has to be put down. It's terrifically corny, but quite moving as well.

'Well, if I start foaming at the mouth,' he said, fully expecting to any minute now, 'don't blame *me*, willya.'

Louie Louie was still busy rubbing his butt from where he'd got it stuck up on the barbed wire. It was only a tiny scratch, but it could have been a lot worse, I guess. Especially if you *can* get lockjaw from it like he said. Either way, it was a hell of an invention, when you thought about it. Barbed wire, I mean. I don't know *who* invented it, or when, or why whoever did invent it thought it was such a great idea that it needed inventing anyway, or why, once he *had* invented it, anyone then thought it'd be just the thing for sticking on top of a wire fence, or across no-man's-land, or all the other places it's ever been used. I guess there's someone some-where who'll think just about anything is a good idea (especially if they thought of it, or can make money out of it), and someone else who'll think of all kinds of ways to make use of it, once it's been invented. Sometimes I actually wonder whether there might have been even worse things invented than those we already know about, but that the inventor, maybe even right on the point of announcing it to the world, suddenly stopped and thought to himself, 'Say, is this such a good idea? Does the world really *need* this? Is it going to make things better or worse?' I'd like to think so, but I doubt it.

'Hey,' said Louie Louie, suddenly stopping rubbing his ass and looking quite nervous. 'I just thought of something. What if this place is guarded by guard dogs?

What if there's a pack of Dobermanns lying in the shadows somewhere just waiting to launch an ambush?'

Louie Louie could always be relied on to come up with a very dramatic scenario. He should have been a dramatist or something. He should have moved to Hollywood and got a job thinking up their crummy plots for them.

'If there *was* a pack of Dobermanns,' I said, 'why the hell would they bother lying in the shadows waiting to ambush us? They're Dobermanns! Why wouldn't they just attack us straight away, while your usually razor-sharp senses were temporarily distracted in fondling your own ass. I mean, if you were a Dobermann, would you be scared of you?'

'I wasn't fondling it,' said Louie Louie, starting to fondle it again. 'I was massaging it. Besides, who says a Dobermann wouldn't be scared of me, anyway?' He was brave as hell all of a sudden now he realised it was pretty unlikely that there *was* a pack of Dobermanns lying in ambush. He was more than ready to take them on now. 'If you wanna know the truth, I wish there *was* a pack of Dobermanns lying in ambush. I'd surprise the be*jeezus* out of them!'

'Sure you would,' I told him. 'They'd wish they'd never been whelped. They'd have to go skulking back to guard-dog school with their tails between their legs.'

'And they wouldn't even be able to do that,' said Louie Louie, 'because they don't even have tails.'

'Sure they do,' I said breezily. 'Little tiny ones. Little goddam stumps of things. They'd have to go skulking back to guard-dog school with their little tiny stumpy tails between their legs.'

'Without so much as a reference!'

''Course not. They'd be fired on the spot.'

'Dereliction of duty.'

'Cowardice in the face of the enemy.'

'Goddam serves them right.'

'Goddam Dobermanns.'

We were out on the pier itself by now. We'd just been strolling along, shooting the bull, not even paying any attention to anything. Louie Louie hadn't started foaming at the mouth yet, and if there really was a pack of Dobermanns lying in ambush somewhere, I guess they must have fallen asleep. Or else they couldn't even be bothered, poor bastards. Anyway, now that we were actually on it, and we realised we were on it, it felt even more rickety than it'd looked. With every step you could hear it creaking and groaning, and we could see the water right through the holes in the boardwalk, where the planks had rotted through. Then I started to imagine what it might be like if the rest of the floorboards suddenly just gave way. If the whole thing suddenly gave way beneath us. I imagined it all in slow motion, too, with us both falling towards that inky blackness. I even thought about how long it might take us to sink, once we hit the water, the shiny slick surface slowly closing over us like wet cement. I could almost imagine how it'd feel. It sent a sudden shiver shooting up my spine, and after that I stepped pretty gingerly, and tried not to look down through any more holes.

'This place is dead as, Daddy-O,' said Louie Louie after a couple of minutes, kicking at a faded tin can. Both the sound of his voice, and especially the tin can, gave me a jolt. To tell you the truth, I was a little jumpy. The whole place was quite spooky, to be honest. It was stripped bare. It'd been picked clean, and what was left was just crumbling away to dust. Like Louie Louie said, it was dead as, Daddy-O, but that was what was kind of interesting about it, too. It was spooky, but like walking-on-the-moon spooky. It was like another world almost. A dead world. Another dimension or something, one we weren't supposed to be able to get to. It was so quiet I could almost hear my own heart beat. Almost.

27

Maybe that was why we got such a surprise when we saw it. We both looked at one another like people do in the movies when they want to make sure the other person has seen whatever it is they've seen, like a beautiful girl walking towards them in the desert, or a card-playing dog or whatever, so they can make sure it's not a mirage or something and that they're not crazy after all. That's exactly how I bet we would've looked to anyone if they'd been there to see us. Like two guys in the movies who think they've just seen a card-playing dog. I guess that's where we got it from in the first place. The movies. People are always picking stuff up from the movies, most of it without even realising it. And when they're not picking it up from actual movies, they're picking it up from other people who have picked it up from movies. Sometimes I think just about everything anybody ever does comes from some movie or other. It's got so that people don't even know how to act any more without copying some character in some stupid movie. I do it myself, *some*times, although I try not to too much. It's very insidious, though. You have to watch out for it. Otherwise, before you even know it, you're walking around half brainwashed, like you're acting in your own private little melodrama or something. Of course, if you *know* you're acting in it, that's one thing. If you don't even realise it, well, boy, that's another.

Anyway, after we'd exchanged looks and everything and established that it wasn't a mirage, or a hallucination or whatever, and that we could both see it, as unbelievable as it was, Louie Louie let out a low whistle. He did this sometimes when he saw something very impressive. Goddam movies again.

'Interesting,' he said.

That was an understatement. Louie Louie was always either overstating or understating. He never got it exactly right. Anyway, what had happened was, we'd reached the very end of the pier, and although it'd been interesting, there really wasn't anything to see. And then we'd just poked our heads through this one door, expecting to find another crummy, falling-down old dilapidated room, with holes in the floor and ceiling, when there it was. At first I didn't even know what I was looking at, it was so unexpected. It just didn't register. Sometimes things don't, if you're not expecting them. I've read that's how the original Americans felt when they first looked out and saw old Christopher Columbus. Standing on the shore, they didn't even know what the hell they were looking at, it was so unexpected. They didn't even know they were looking at *any*thing. They learned pretty quick, though. Then, to use a rather apt expression, what happened was the penny dropped. I suddenly realised what it was I was looking at. All the mixed-up, jumbled-up bits had taken recognisable shape all of a sudden inside my head. It probably only took about a second in reality, but at the time it felt much longer. It felt like I'd been staring at it and trying to figure out what it was for a long time. And that's when the penny dropped, and the reason I said it was apt was because what had taken shape inside my head was an old penny arcade. If you don't know what one is, it's a bit hard to explain, so I'll just assume you do and not even try. It's not that I can't be bothered, it's just that I'm lousy at describing things. I really am. I stink. My descriptive powers are very weak. Anyway, that's what it was. It was perfectly preserved in every detail, too, like it was an exhibit in a museum. It looked like time had just stopped. Just like that. Why it had stopped there, and nowhere else, I don't know, but the whole place was like a time capsule. There were even a couple of glass display cases full of old faded magazines and newspapers, as if they were still for sale, full of old news that not even the oldest person in the world would be able to remember. There was so much news nowadays, round the clock, it was kind of strange to think that this particular news, whether it was some big deal or not, was still just sitting there, waiting to be read, as if it had only just happened the day before. It was kind of sad, too, in a way, because it never *would* be read, not now. It reminded me a bit of a little kid with a secret but no one to tell. Standing there at the doorway like that, I suddenly felt I was on the verge of some big discovery, like old Howard Carter about to enter King Tut's tomb or something. I'm crazy about that stuff. Egyptology. An archaeologist is really something I wouldn't have minded being. I think it would be quite interesting. Anyhow, that's how I felt. On the brink of something just waiting to be discovered. Somehow it had survived, its seals intact. It had remained secret and hidden.

'Well?' I said.

'Well, what?' said Louie Louie.

'Well, what are we waiting for?'

We were still standing in the doorway. We hadn't even moved. It was like we weren't sure whether we should or not, whether we might be intruding. The place looked like it was sleeping and we weren't sure whether we should disturb it. Whether we *wanted* to disturb it even. It was funny. Actually, I don't know what we were waiting for. But Louie Louie's naturally suspicious mind was already at work.

'What if it's a trap?' he said. Maybe he was still thinking about those Dobermanns lying outside somewhere in ambush.

'What kind of a trap?'

'How should I know? If I knew that, it wouldn't be a trap, would it?'

'Yes, it would.' I was being all pedantic all of a sudden, which is something I hate. 'It'd still be a trap. You'd just know what *kind* of a trap, that's all. Knowing what kind of a trap a trap is doesn't not make it a trap,' I told him.

We both just stood there some more, looking at each other, waiting for the other one to decide what the hell to do. We were both wearing these very serious expressions the whole time, like we were on opposing debating teams or something. We might have been debating some very serious topic such as the merits or otherwise of the Geneva Convention by the looks on our faces. The Geneva Convention, just in case you've never heard of it, was this set of rules about what you could and couldn't do during a war. Imagine that.

'Bet you can't say that three times in a goddam row,' said Louie Louie.

'Say what?'

'What you just said. I bet you can't say what you just said three times in a row.'

'Bet I can.'

'Five bucks?'

'Make it ten.'

'Deal.'

'Dammit!' I said, about five seconds later. 'I can't even remember what I said in the first place.'

'I think you said you owe me ten bucks.'

Goddam Louie Louie. It cost me ten bucks, but horsing around like that changed our mood completely. Sometimes that's all it takes. If I hadn't said what I'd said in that very ridiculous way without even meaning to, and if Louie Louie hadn't picked up on it the way he did, and said what he said with such a straight face, we might not even have gone inside. We might not even have felt like it, although we probably would have. I'm pretty certain we would have. We wouldn't have been so exuberant about it, though, that's for sure. We'd probably have been quite subdued, and tiptoed about the place like it was a fusty old museum or something, at least at first. As it was, we were suddenly in very high spirits, just from a little horsing around. We weren't bothered in the least about intruding or disturbing things. We were like a couple of little kids on Christmas Day who have just woken up and remembered it's Christmas Day. I remember that actually happening once or twice. You'd think that that'd be the last thing a little kid would ever forget, but I'm sure it happens all the time. And the thing is, when you *have* forgotten something like that, it makes it even better when you remember it again.

When you remember it, something like that, like it's Christmas Day, or your birthday, or that it's the first day of the holidays or whatever, it's just about the best feeling in the world.

The first thing we did once we were inside was we helped ourselves to a couple of big handfuls of old pennies. They were sitting in this very ornate old till we found which was full of them. We just stuffed them in our pockets like treasure. We figured it was okay, and not stealing or anything, because all we were going to do was feed them straight back into the machines again anyway. Besides, I think we actually kind of regarded it as treasure, like a pirate's chest of Spanish doubloons, and as such finders keepers. We even let them run through our fingers a few times, enjoying the feel of them, even if they were only old pennies and not pieces of eight.

Then we turned our attention to the various machines themselves. We didn't know where to start. They were all lined up in rows, very neatly, and against the walls. There must have been about twenty or thirty of them altogether. They were quite simple, most of them, but very well made and very intriguing-looking. I guess they were spring-activated, or else clockwork, although there were a few that looked like they might have run on electricity. And when I say they were well made, I mean the woodwork, I guess, and all the little details. Everything was very beautifully finished. It really was. All the little knobs and handles and buttons and moving parts and everything. They looked like a lot of attention had been paid to them. You could quite easily have just stuck one in your house as an ornament or something. If you did, I'm sure people would just admire the hell out of it too.

I'm not kidding. Plus, it'd give you something to do. You could turn off the lousy television once in a while. And not only were they very well made and attractive-looking in their own right, but they turned out to be a lot of fun as well. Actually, they were a riot. You mightn't think so to look at them, but they were. They were so much fun we nearly killed ourselves. We couldn't shove the pennies into the slots fast enough, laughing our heads off like a couple of lunatics. Actually, I think we might have been a little hysterical, if you want to know the truth. They were a lot of fun, but not *that* much fun. After all that eerie silence and those unread newspapers and empty boardwalks and everything, I guess we just wanted to make as much noise as possible. We wanted to release a little tension.

Whenever we ran out of pennies we just helped ourselves to more. The old till was full of them. At first we were practically running from one machine to the next, like a couple of hyperactive kids, we were that excited. But then, after I don't know how long, I came across this one particular machine that really caught my attention. It was called Haunted House, and was towards the back of the room. We might have been in there twenty minutes by then or it might have been two hours. It was hard to say. At first glance it didn't seem all that interesting, but once I'd stopped to take a good look at it, I became quite intrigued. It was an old wooden cabinet (very well made) with a glass front, about four feet high. Inside there was a kind of tableau, a model of an old-fashioned bedroom with a tiny bed, a chair either side of it, a small ornate chandelier hanging from the ceiling, a high bookcase against one wall (with incredibly tiny, individually painted books) and a curtained French window at the back. A little hand-painted figure was lying in the bed, clutching the covers, and another one sitting in each of the chairs either side of it. It was one of the few machines that ran on electricity, and in fact someone must have only just put a coin in when the plug was pulled, because the little scene was frozen in time, halfway through its spooky performance. The little bed was suspended just above the floor, like it was levitating or something. A creepy gnarled hand had half reached round the curtained French window, perhaps about to draw it back, and the bookcase, which was directly opposite the bed, had swung away from the wall, half revealing a darkened passageway beyond. I know it doesn't sound particularly fascinating, but for some reason it was. I don't know why. It was also quite spooky, although, once again, I couldn't say why. It just was. And the passageway was the spookiest thing of all. It actually gave me the shivers. In fact, I was just about to turn away and take a look at something else because it was giving me the shivers so much when I noticed something odd about it. A faint orange glow had started pulsing just out of sight, as if the passageway was real, and actually continued on someplace, and the light was just around the bend. It was odd because of course there was no bend. The passageway was only painted on.

I stared at it, transfixed. It really was the oddest thing. I couldn't figure it out. And then, I swear, what happened next was it started getting brighter. It started pulsing brighter and brighter. But then I suddenly thought, with a really terrible case of the creeps, what if it wasn't getting *bright*er, but *close*r. What if it was just getting closer and closer, creeping up that tiny, darkened, painted passageway.

'God*dam*!' cried Louie Louie suddenly, from where he was playing another machine somewhere behind me. He nearly made me jump out of my skin. I really nearly had a heart attack when he said it, I was so tense. 'You gotta see this, Montanna! *Boy!*'

At the sound of his voice, apart from nearly having a heart attack, I naturally glanced up. I couldn't help it. It was only for a second, but when I looked back, guess what? The goodam bookcase was closed.

28

What had got Louie Louie so worked up was he'd found a very ancient peep show called What the Butler Saw. They were the kind of things that people, once upon a time, would pretend not to have any interest in whatsoever while they went about playing all the other machines, but that as soon as they thought no one was looking they'd almost break their necks to have a turn on. I guess just about the most embarrassing thing that could happen to a person back then was to be discovered furtively enjoying What the Butler Saw. It was probably okay if you were looking at it in a sort of ironical way, though, even if you really weren't. I guess that might have been okay. You can get away with a lot of stuff if you're being ironical about it, or pretending to be. For some reason it just seems to help. Not that Louie Louie was. He wasn't even pretending. He was more like a dirty old man, his eyes glued to the viewfinder, while he cranked the old handle round and round, making the photos inside flip faster and faster. That's how it worked. The faster you cranked the handle, the faster the photos flipped, making whatever it was you were looking at appear to move, just like a regular movie. By the look on Louie Louie's face, whatever he was looking at must have been something pretty sexy. By the look on his face, maybe it was Miss America in there or somebody. Maybe she was giving him the big come-on or something.

'Holy cow!' he said, grinning and leering like a sexy village idiot or somebody. He wouldn't have cared if there'd been a whole roomful of people watching him. He wouldn't have cared a damn. 'This is hot stuff! Boy, oh boy! This girl is something else, Montanna! You really oughta take a look. It'll really open your eyes, young kid like you.' All the while he was saying this he was still turning the handle round and round. He hadn't even looked up, he was so engrossed. Then it must have come to the end and he stopped cranking. 'Actually, on second thoughts,' he said, looking up at last, 'maybe you better not take a look after all. You might not be able to handle it. Kid like you. I'd hate to see you bug-eyed for life.'

'Like you, you mean?'

'Ho, goddam ho,' he said. 'Well, better bug-eyed than bug-brained.'

'Better bug-brained than *pea*-brained.'

'Better pea-brained than peed *on*.'

He was so tickled by his own joke, which wasn't a bad one, that he was still chuckling over it as he stood aside to let me take my place at the machine. I wasn't really that interested, but I shoved a penny in and took a look anyway. Trying to feel as ironical as I could, I pressed my eyes up against the viewfinder and peered in, back through time, back through the years, at the faded old photograph inside. It was impossible to tell how old it was, but it was old, all sepia-toned and sort of stained around the edges. It was a picture of a slightly chubby young woman, with small breasts and a shy smile. For some reason, that smile really got me. It was really a nice smile, even though it was actually probably more nervous than shy, now that I think about it. To tell you the truth, she looked pretty apprehensive about the whole thing, like maybe she was just beginning to wonder whether it was such a great idea after all, taking all her clothes off for that nice young man she'd just met, with his newfangled camera contraption. I was already feeling pretty sorry for her, to tell you the truth. I really was. I was also finding it quite difficult to feel or look even a little ironical.

But then I started turning the handle anyway and the photo clicked over, replaced by another, almost identical one. Same shy – or apprehensive – smile. I turned the handle faster and the photos clicked past faster, the naked, chubby woman beginning to dance clumsily before my eyes. Boy, she was no dancer, that's for sure. It was pretty pathetic. No kidding. Of course, I didn't know the woman's story or anything, but I felt sorry for her all the same. I felt it probably wasn't exactly the sort of thing she'd imagined she'd be doing when she grew up, back when she was a kid or whenever. It might have been, but I doubted it. And the more she danced, the worse I started to feel about the whole thing. I wished I'd never even taken a look. But the thing is, I already knew I was going to feel like that even before I took a look. I just knew it. But I looked anyway, and now I was feeling terrible about it. Serves me right. Then I noticed something kind of odd happening. It was a day of odd things, I guess, but I wasn't thinking about it like that. I wasn't putting them

115

together or anything. They just happened. And now this. The chubby young woman was still dancing in front of me, but she wasn't just moving through space any more. She was moving through time as well. I mean she was growing older. She started ageing right in front of me. Her smooth, plump body started to sag and wrinkle right before my eyes. Her hair started to grow long and thin and then her teeth just rotted all to hell and fell out. The most horrible thing, though, was that she kept right on smiling and dancing, even when her bones started poking right through her paper-thin skin. Then, finally, she just crumpled all to dust. Then the viewfinder went black.

My hand suddenly stopped winding the handle, but I couldn't let go of it yet. I'd been holding on to it so tightly I couldn't unclench it. And it was only then, once I'd stopped winding it, that I remembered I'd even been doing it. I'd been winding that damn handle the whole time and I hadn't even realised it. And that's when I realised something else. It suddenly occurred to me that maybe I could have stopped it. Maybe I could have stopped it if I'd only just stopped turning that damn handle.

'Oh brother,' said Louie Louie, still leering like crazy. He was like a sex maniac or something. He really was. 'I wouldn't mind showing her a good time! I'd really give her something to smile about. Goddam sweetie.'

For some reason I was suddenly mad as hell at that.

'Louie Louie,' I said, 'you're a goddam sick pervert, d'ya know that? I goddam mean it.'

It wasn't the reaction he was expecting, but he was

delighted. Insults were like water off a duck's back to him. You couldn't hurt his feelings with a baseball bat. He didn't know what had done it or why, but he could tell something had really irritated me. He could tell that something had really got under my skin.

'Wuddaya mean me?' he protested. 'You're the one drooling all over the crummy machine. Man, you oughta be ashamed of yourself, Montanna. You really ought. Ogling your own grandmother like that.'

I'm not a violent person, but I could've socked him. I really could. And it wasn't because of the grandmother remark, either. Hell, if my grandmother was anything like my mother, it wouldn't surprise me a bit if it *was* her.

'Louie Louie,' I told him, 'I oughta knock your teeth in!'

Louie Louie was enjoying himself tremendously by this stage. As far as he was concerned, all he'd done was make one little innocent observation about how he wouldn't mind showing someone a good time, and for some reason I'd gone and exploded. He couldn't believe his luck.

'Boy, oh boy!' he said. 'That must be some big hair you've got up your ass!'

I was so mad now I could hardly stand it. I was almost in a goddam rage or something. 'No *hair*!' I said, and even as I said it I knew how dumb I must have sounded. I must have sounded like a real stinking moron. 'No *hair*!' I said again, just so there wouldn't be any doubt about how big a moron I was. 'I just think you should show a bit more goddam respect sometimes. *That's* all.'

When I said that Louie Louie suddenly became all serious. Anyone who didn't know him might have thought he was really considering what I'd just said, about showing more respect, to look at him. He looked so straight-faced and thoughtful that he might have been actually really considering it.

'Hell, maybe you're right, Montanna,' he said. He looked quite contrite all of a sudden. Like he was a little bit ashamed of himself. 'Maybe I should show a bit more respect. Maybe I am, just like you say, a goddam sick pervert. It wouldn't surprise me a bit. It really wouldn't.' Boy, he really looked like he meant it. I almost believed it myself. What an actor. 'But *Jeez Louize*, it sure sounds like you've got a hair up your ass to me.'

I guess he was right. I guess maybe I did have a hair up my ass, whatever that means. I didn't know it, but I guess I did.

I wasn't really mad any more, though. I'd calmed down a lot. 'Louie Louie –' I said, but just then there was a sudden creaking noise behind us, and we both spun around. It was the first sound we'd heard that we hadn't made ourselves. It made us both jump. All it was, though, was a faded old metal sign swinging from the wall by a screw. A second screw was on the floor beneath it, where it must have just fallen, I suppose, although we hadn't heard it. Not that we would have, just a screw coming loose. I couldn't quite make out what the sign said.

'Let's get the hell out of here,' I suggested.

'What's the matter?' Louie Louie asked. 'Spooked?'

'I would be if I had a face like yours,' I told him. 'Every time I looked in the goddam mirror.'

Louie Louie held his sides very sarcastically. He said, 'Did I ever tell you you just kill me sometimes?'

29

Of course, I didn't let on to Louie Louie that he was right, that I *was* a bit spooked, but I was. To be honest, I was pretty glad to get the hell out of there, although naturally I acted as cool as could be. What I did was, once we'd got back outside again, I just kind of strolled along, back the way we'd come, as if nothing the least bit out of the ordinary had even happened. I just stuck my hands in my pockets and tried to look as non-chalant as somebody out for an afternoon stroll, although I definitely didn't feel it. I was pretending my head off. I probably would have tried whistling, except I can't even whistle.

We didn't say two words the whole time. I don't know why exactly. We just didn't feel like it. And then, once we'd renegotiated the fence, this time without anyone – that is, Louie Louie – getting stuck, we drifted back to the stretch of beach where we'd been before. In fact, we ended up back at the exact same spot, where our shapes in the sand looked like they were waiting for us. Louie Louie climbed back into his and was soon stretched out like he was at a five-star resort, taking a break between rum punches served up in coconut cups. He was really taking it easy. Wherever he was, he had a knack for getting comfortable. He was a genius at it.

Although neither one of us had felt much like talking before, after we'd first come out of the arcade, and I still didn't feel like it, Louie Louie for some reason really felt like shooting the bull all of a sudden. He started talking about zombie movies, or some damn thing, although to tell you the truth I wasn't really listening. He was excited as hell about it, though.

'So?' he said at last, in this very excited, expectant voice, after what might have been five minutes or an hour, for all I knew. 'Wuddaya think?'

I looked at him blankly. 'About what?' I said, which really annoyed him.

'About my goddam zombie movie, that's what.' He'd got himself all worked up telling me about his great movie idea and I hadn't even been listening. He thought his ideas were so great he couldn't believe anyone wouldn't be on the edge of their seat listening to one of them. They *were* pretty good too.

'Oh, that,' I said, then pretended to think about it for a minute. Then I said, 'I think it stinks,' which *really* annoyed him.

He let out a terrific snort. It was supposed to be very contemptuous, I guess, but it sounded like he was only clearing his nasal passages or something. 'Well, then,' he said, very snootily, 'it's obvious you wouldn't know a good zombie movie if one bit you on your ass!'

30

He was right too. I wouldn't. I definitely wasn't an authority on the genre. To be honest, I'm not overly crazy about zombie movies. I have a very weak stomach for that kind of thing. It's very easily unsettled. And it's no good my telling myself it's only a movie, either, when someone's just about to have their face bitten off or something. I *know* it's only a movie. I'm not a moron. Plus I hate it when people do that. I've actually known one or two guys that were always doing it. 'It's only a stupid movie,' they'd say, every time anyone started discussing a movie in earnest, especially when they started discussing what might have happened after the movie finished. To the characters, I mean. Of course everyone *knows* nothing happens to them. They're just characters. But people still like to imagine what they might have gone on and done after the events portrayed in the movie. It's only natural. In fact, if you come out of a movie and you're *not* wondering about it, then it probably wasn't a very good movie. Obviously the actors all just go home again, or else start making another movie, or get divorced and marry their co-star, or maybe just go on an eating binge or something. They're almost like real people – the actors, I mean – only more self-important. But anyway, even though I *know* it's only a movie, my stomach still gets unsettled all the same. I guess I'm just more of a shadows and fog fan. So as I say, Louie Louie was probably right. I probably wouldn't know a good zombie movie if one bit me on my ass. But also, I only said his movie stank to rile him. In fact, from what I'd heard it actually sounded like a pretty good idea.

It was a zombie movie *about* a zombie movie, where during the movie within a movie (which would be a very big deal, and would be simultaneously premiering all over the world) the zombie characters would come alive, literally. They'd literally step out of the movie and into the audience, with all the usual ensuing zombie movie mayhem. But the really clever part was that while the audience was watching it – the real audience, I mean – while they were sitting there in the dark watching those zombies step out of the movie within a movie into the audience, they'd be nervously thinking, 'Boy, I hope those goddam zombies don't *really* start stepping out of the movie!' They'd all be nervous as hell, and really enjoying themselves thinking they might really do it. That is, providing some sonuvabitch beside them didn't lean over at some crucial stage and whisper 'Don't worry, it's only a stupid movie' in their ear.

The other thing, though, is I'd been busy watching something in the distance. All it was was a tiny speck further along the beach, that was all. No big deal. I couldn't even tell what it was, but I kept watching it all the same. That was why I hadn't exactly been following all the specific details of Louie Louie's plot. Whatever it was, though, it was coming towards us, or *appeared* to be, without actually moving. What I mean is, while I was watching it, it wouldn't do anything. It'd just be there. But then, no matter how hard I tried, my concentration would somehow or other suddenly lapse, or else I'd just blink or something, and then there it would be, that little bit closer. Actually, when I say my concentration would somehow or other suddenly lapse, that's not quite right. What would happen was, every so often, out of the corner of my eye, I thought I could catch a glimpse of that faint orange glow again, the one from the secret passageway, pulsing gently just out of sight. And when I looked back, the tiny speck would be a little closer.

After Louie Louie had told me I wouldn't know a good zombie movie if one bit me on the ass, and I'd agreed with him, I went back to watching the speck. I suddenly felt like I'd had my eyes off it long enough. It was already quite a bit closer, although I still couldn't make it out. My eyes aren't really that fantastic, if you want to know the truth. I mean, they're okay, but not fantastic. Actually, I don't know if they're any worse than anyone else's, but they could definitely be better. I don't mean I need glasses or anything, it's just that I've never really been able to see things as clearly as I'd have liked. I've always wished I could see things how an eagle or something with very keen eyesight sees things, with this very clear, penetrating gaze. I've always thought that that would help a lot. Meanwhile Louie Louie, who was still sulking about his movie, hadn't even noticed it yet, whatever it was, and for some reason I didn't want to draw his attention to it. I was determined to ignore the orange glow from now on and just concentrate like crazy on that strange speck. I was determined not to take my eyes off it, not even to blink. I figured that if I did that then maybe it wouldn't get any closer. I didn't know why, but I wasn't sure I wanted it to get any closer. But as hard as I concentrated, and as unblinkingly as I stared, that orange glow wasn't so easy to ignore. Again and again it would catch me out until, before I knew it, the tiny speck wasn't so tiny any more. In fact, it wasn't a speck at all – it was a person. A crazy old lady pushing a crazy old pram full of babies. Or at least, at first I thought they were babies, but they weren't. They were just a bunch of creepy old dolls, all oversized heads and empty eye sockets.

Louie Louie noticed her now for the first time, now that she was right in front of his face, between us and the sea. That was when he usually noticed things. She was probably only thirty feet away. I don't know how he hadn't seen her before. I guess she must've crept up on his blind spot or something. He nearly jumped out of his skin, though, when he did.

'Jesus, Montanna!' he said. 'She nearly gave me a heart attack. Where'd she spring from anyway?'

'I guess she must have materialised out of thin air,' I told him.

'With a pram?' Then he noticed what was in it. 'Jesus!' he said again. 'What's she got in there? Babies?'

'Dolls,' I told him.

'Dolls? What is she, crazy or something?'

'Looks like it.'

It wasn't easy work through the sand, even right by the shore, where it was firmer, but she struggled along all the same, determined to get someplace, or more likely no place in particular. The wheels ploughed two long ruts behind her, leaving a crazy old trail like the thread of the unintelligible conversation she was having with herself, or maybe with her crazy old dolls. I wondered how far back those ruts went. How many miles and how many years.

'Who the hell is she, d'ya suppose?' Louie Louie asked.

'Goddam bag lady, I guess.'

'*Pram* lady, you mean.' We just watched her for a while. 'What does she want with so many dolls, anyway?'

'I don't know, Louie Louie. Why don't you go and ask her,' I suggested. Louie Louie was like that. He was always asking you a thousand questions about things you had no more idea about than he did. If you were watching a movie with him, for example, even though neither one of you had ever seen it before, he'd be forever asking you stuff like 'Who's that guy?' or 'What did he do that for?' or 'Where's he going now?' or *some*thing. Sometimes I'd just make stuff up and tell him that. By the end of the movie he'd be so confused after trying to reconcile whatever fantastical plot I'd concocted with whatever was actually happening on-screen he wouldn't have the first clue what it was about. 'Perhaps she'll let you take one home to play with,' I told him.

I was being all jokey about it, but I didn't feel it. I was only being like that because the old lady looked so crazy and pathetic and she'd just suddenly appeared like she did. She looked about a hundred and ten years old or something, maybe older, and was wearing this very thin, threadbare old nightshirt, very ragged round the edges and hanging to her knees. On her feet she was wearing a pair of ruby red slippers, and as Louie Louie and I just sat there, close enough to hear her crazy muttering, I don't know what he was thinking, but I was thinking, 'I wonder if she knows all she has to do

126

is click them together?' And then, just as she came right up level with us, and in spite of what I said earlier about it being dead and everything in it being dead, an enormous sea monster of vaguely slug-like appearance burst out of the inky sludge and landed right on top of her.

31

She never even saw it coming. She might have done, if she hadn't just turned towards us, Louie Louie and me, where we were sitting amongst the refuse and junk. I don't know whether she'd only just spotted us or whether she'd been watching *my* speck the same as I'd been watching *hers*. She'd only just turned towards us, anyway. She'd just stopped, turned towards us, then opened her toothless old mouth to speak. She was close enough for us to see the crazy smudged lipstick all around it. It looked like a cave. I half expected a swarm of tiny bats to come flying out of it. But apparently she had something to say to us, something she wanted to communicate. Whatever it was, I'd already decided that it was of the utmost importance. She was in the very act of forming a word, about to breathe life into it, when –

Splat!

Louie Louie and I just sat there, staring at the great quivering mass lying on the spot where the old lady had been. It was probably the perfect opportunity to exchange another one of those corny movie looks I was talking about, to make sure we'd both seen whatever it was we thought we'd seen, but we didn't. I guess we didn't think of it. Then, after I don't know how long, Louie Louie said, 'Goddam.' Then he said it again. 'Goddam.' There wasn't much else to say.

We got up, but slowly. We weren't in any big rush to

go any closer. We weren't exactly breaking our necks or anything about it. But then our curiosity got the better of us, and also we knew we couldn't just stand there and *not* take a look, so we made our way down to the disgusting blob, where it sat, motionless except for that slight quivering, half in, half out of the stinking sludge. There was no sign of the old lady and her pram. Her crazy trail in the sand ended where the monster began. At first we just studied it for a while, not too close, but edging closer and closer. We were really being brave as hell about it. No kidding. Then after it didn't look like doing anything, I picked up a stick and tried giving it a tentative prod. I'd expected it to be hard and leathery, but it went straight in like a hot poker through marshmallow. So then I started wiggling it around a bit, creating a great gash in the monster's side. It kind of quivered all over at that.

'What the hell is it?' asked Louie Louie.

'Dunno,' I said. 'Goddam sea monster, I guess.'

'No such thing,' said Louie Louie.

'Sez who?'

'Sez me. Sez everyone.'

'Then what the hell is it?' I asked him.

'Dunno,' he said. 'Goddam sea monster, I guess.'

Not knowing what else to do, we stood there for a while, just kind of studying it some more. We walked around it. We peered at it. Louie Louie even sniffed at it. 'Stinks!' he said. We were trying to make sense of something that made no sense.

'Poor old crazy bag lady,' I said.

'Poor old crazy *pram* lady,' said Louie Louie. 'Didn't even see it coming.'

'I wonder what she was going to say?' I was thinking about how she'd turned to us, just before it happened. How she'd been about to say something.

'Hello, I guess. Just being friendly.'

I didn't say anything, but like I said, I wasn't so sure. I had a feeling there was more to it than that. I didn't know what, but something. I wished I could have got to hear what she'd had to say, that was all. I wished she'd got to say it. But then I thought I heard something.

'What was that?' I said, listening.

'What was what?' asked Louie Louie.

'I thought I heard something. In *there*.' I indicated the hole I'd ripped in the monster's side.

'In *there*?' he repeated incredulously. He put his ear to the hole and listened. 'You're nuts,' he said.

But I was sure I'd heard something. I didn't know what, but something. I dug around with the stick some more in the hole I'd already made, making it bigger. The monster started quivering again, but I ignored it. I wasn't thinking of the monster at all. I just kept on probing about with that old stick, making the hole bigger and bigger. Pretty soon it was almost big enough to crawl right into. Then I heard it again, still muffled and faint, but louder than before.

'Can you hear it now?' I said, getting all excited.

I didn't even wait for his answer. I just threw the stick away and started digging into the soft, gelatinous flesh with my hands, scooping out great handfuls of the stuff. The deeper I went, the softer it got, and the monster began to shudder and groan. Maybe the softer stuff was the equivalent of its vital organs or something. If it was, I didn't even care. I just kept digging. I could hear something now like the sound of water sucking at sand, and something else like water-logged lungs desperately gasping for air.

Then I saw her, just for a second, before the space I'd scooped out filled up again with liquid guts. The crazy old lady. Her mouth was open, screaming, a hole in a shrunken head. A black tunnel to nowhere, to nothing. A cave. A swarm of tiny bats spewed out, and with a sound like a couple of thousand gallons of wet cement being sucked round an S-bend, the sea monster – crazy old lady, pram and all – was gone.

32

I guess old Louie Louie was probably some sort of goddam hero. I guess I owed him my life or something. I mean, if he hadn't grabbed hold of me when he did, pulling me clear in the nick of time, maybe I'd have disappeared back into the sludge as well. Maybe I'd have been carried down to the bottom of that dead sea. Maybe I'd be there now. As it was, he did and I wasn't. He was a regular real-life life-saver, no doubt about it, and if I didn't say it at the time, thanks, Louie Louie. I mean it. You're a pal.

I was left feeling pretty stunned, I guess, as well as covered from head to foot in a strange, foamy scum, the fast-evaporating flesh of the sea monster. I was coated in it. Within seconds, however, even this was gone.

'Montanna, you crazy sonuvabitch!' We were still sitting in the sand where we'd fallen after he'd pulled me free. 'You nearly got swallowed *whole*! Jesus Christ! What the hell were you doing in there, anyway? Looking for your goddam marbles?'

Maybe I was. I don't know. Anyway, the sea monster was gone. It had disappeared back to wherever it had come from. Maybe it'd even got what it had come for. Who the hell knows? I just sat there looking at the sea. To look at it, you'd think it was dead. Anyone would. You'd think there wasn't a single living thing in there, but you'd be wrong.

But now I noticed there was something half buried in the sand where the sea monster had been. I couldn't make it out, but it was something. Without saying anything, I got up to take a look. I was curious as hell all of a sudden. I really wondered what it could be. I thought it might be a clue or something. Louie Louie didn't say anything either. He was just sitting in the sand watching me, probably still thinking I'd lost my marbles. I wouldn't blame him if he was. When I got to whatever it was buried in the sand I bent down to take a closer look. It was only an old wooden box, a bit bigger than a shoebox, but with a bunch of knobs and switches on it, like a control panel. There were also all kinds of other crazy attachments I couldn't figure out. Wires and electrodes and what looked like maybe finger clamps. It was making a soft humming sound.

I held out a hand to touch it.

'*Don't!*'

Louie Louie was standing beside me. He'd grabbed hold of my arm, was still holding it, in fact. When I looked up at him he looked embarrassed and let it go.

'I mean, you don't want to get an electric shock or anything, do you?' he said.

'Don't worry, Mom,' I told him. 'I'll be careful.'

It was warm to the touch, and thrummed gently under my palm. I could feel a soft liquid current flowing out of it and up my arm, making the fine short hairs stand to attention along its path. Before it could reach any further, though, I snapped my hand away.

'Didja get a shock?' asked Louie Louie hopefully.

But I didn't reply. I'd heard him, but I was too busy wondering why I'd pulled my hand away so suddenly.

What did I think was going to happen, anyway? The current hadn't been unpleasant, in fact, almost the opposite. It had felt strangely soothing, almost alive, like a caress.

But Louie Louie was waiting.

'*Well?*' he said.

'Well, what?'

'Well, *what* then?'

I shrugged.

'Nothing,' I said.

'Nothing? Huh.'

He looked at the crazy box again. He still looked a little dubious, to tell the truth, but he reached out and touched it anyway, as tentatively as hell, like he was half expecting it to bite him or something. He snatched his hand back, instantly, obviously expecting it to be hot, then returned it when he realised it wasn't.

'Nothing,' he said, disappointed. 'Not even warm.'

33

Naturally we reported it to the police. The old lady, I mean. She may only have been some crazy old lady, but for all we knew she might have had some crazy old husband someplace, sitting at home doing his own crazy stuff, but worried sick all the same. She might even have had some *not*-so-crazy relatives. Sons and daughters and nieces and nephews and even grand-children. If so, we figured they ought to at least know what had happened to her, even though they probably wouldn't be too thrilled about it. Nobody would be. Of course, I didn't give the police all the details. The stuff about hacking my way inside the monster to find her and everything. I didn't think her relatives, *if* she had any, probably needed to know about that part. If she *did* have some not-so-crazy relatives after all, it was probably going to be difficult enough to deal with as it was. So we reported it to the police, but left a few things out. We went to the nearest police station and told a guy on the front desk what we'd seen, and what he did was, he just sat there, listening and cracking his hairy knuckles, and although it was a pretty fantastic story, even without all the details, his expression didn't change once. That's the problem with some people. They're so hard to impress it's not even worth trying. And the reason they're so hard to impress isn't, as you might think, because they've already seen and heard everything, but because they've got no imagination. Life's just one long things-to-do list for people like that. As for the knuckle-cracking, well, some people are just knuckle-cracking addicts. I know this from experience because I actually went through a knuckle-cracking phase myself. Finally it got to the point where I was doing it all the time, so I just gave it up. Also, it can actually drive some people nuts. I don't mean the person doing it, of course, I mean other people. Personally, I think neck-cracking's the worst. I used to do that too, but quit after I cracked it one time and it got stuck in a sideways position. I had to walk around everywhere sideways for a week, like an ancient Egyptian, so as not to bump into things. But there was something else about this guy apart from his obvious lack of imagination and knuckle-cracking. They were bad enough, but this other thing was a hundred times worse. I guess it wasn't his fault, but he had four thumbs. Two on each hand. It really was the creepiest damn thing. And guess what, he cracked these too.

Actually he wasn't the first four-thumbed guy I'd ever seen. I once saw a guy on top of the Empire State Building, of all places, who also had four thumbs. At least, I'm guessing he had four. I only actually got a good look at his one hand, but it certainly had two. I was only a little kid, on a school excursion, which means Louie Louie must have been around someplace, although he never saw the guy, or what he did next, which has always been a bit of a sore point. Louie Louie has always hated not seeing stuff like that. If you've seen something, and he hasn't, he can actually take it quite personally, like it was your fault. He'll even hold it against you. And back then I had a pretty good eye for anything unusual. I was always spotting stuff and then pointing it out to whoever the hell was nearby. It didn't even matter whether I knew them or not. It was only later I realised that that was just the kind of stuff you weren't supposed to point out, but I didn't know that then. I actually thought the opposite was true, that it was my duty or something. That anything out of the ordinary needed pointing out. Anyway, I was just about to bring this particular little curio to public attention, the fact that this guy had two, or possibly four thumbs, when all of a sudden, someone screamed.

There's nothing quite like a scream, especially if it's really piercing and unexpected, for getting people's attention. People will drop just about anything when they hear a really good scream. I guess it goes back thousands of years to when we were all goddam apes, or near as. When someone screamed back then, I guess they probably had a pretty good reason for doing it, so it was worthwhile paying attention. Now everyone turned and stared at the woman who'd just screamed, including me. Sometimes you'll hear a scream, especially if it's one of those really high-pitched kids' screams they let out when they're excited or angry or just for the hell of it, and it makes you want to strangle the kid on the spot, it's so high and shrill. Well, this wasn't like that. This was the kind of scream that when you heard it you just knew that something was wrong. So it wasn't long before everyone's attention turned from the woman who'd screamed, to what she'd screamed *about*. It was the four-thumbed guy, who I hadn't even had a chance to point out yet. What he'd done was he'd somehow climbed out onto the wrong side of the safety railing, eighty-six floors up, although how he'd managed to do it so quick I couldn't say. I must've only turned away for a couple of seconds, looking for someone to blab to about his four thumbs. He was holding on with one hand, as calm as can be, like he was riding a tram or something. Like he was Gene Kelly or somebody holding on to a lamp post. After that first scream, although you'd think there would have been, there wasn't another sound, not for what seemed the longest time. Even the people who'd heard it but couldn't see the guy because they were on the other side or were too short or whatever didn't make a sound. Everyone just seemed to kind of hold their breath, waiting to see what'd happen next. It was probably only a second or two but it seemed much longer.

Then he just let go.

He didn't make a sound, either, didn't scream or yell or anything, just toppled out of view.

About the exact same time as he let go, though, there was another scream, and although I guess it wasn't so unexpected this time, it was about ten thousand times worse than the first one. It was a different kind of scream altogether. Whereas the first one had been piercing and unexpected, and told you that something was wrong, this one was just kind of bottomless, a bottomless scream. It didn't tell you something was wrong, it told you something too terrible for words had already happened. The terrible thing, whatever it was, couldn't be undone. And then she just wouldn't stop screaming, the woman who'd screamed, and each scream, believe it or not, was worse than the one before, until people were actually covering their ears with their hands. They couldn't stand it. But it was no use. Her screams were contagious. In no time at all one person after another became infected, whether they'd covered their ears or not, and then they'd start screaming too. Of course, when people first realised what was happening they started rushing for the exit, but I guess someone must have tripped, and then everyone tripped over them, and then it was just too late. And pretty soon just about everyone on the observation deck was screaming, myself included. Even Louie Louie, who hadn't even seen anything, was screaming. And all the while more and more people were coming up to see what all the screaming was about, and of course they'd start screaming as well. Then what happened was all our screams started drifting out over the city, infecting all the people down on the streets, and in the cars and taxis. They even seeped into the subway and onto the trains, and snuck past doormen, into buildings. They travelled up and down elevators, infecting whole office and apartment blocks, and pretty soon there were carloads of screaming people crossing the Brooklyn Bridge, heading for Long Island, and across the Hudson, into Jersey. From there I guess it just kept on spreading, maybe right across the country, maybe right across the world. Eventually a state of emergency was declared.

The loudest screamers were rounded up and shot – for the greater good, of course. The government explained everything. And in a way it did the trick. Soon people learned to scream on the inside again, and things could get back to normal.

Once we'd finished telling the cop our story, he said, 'You've done the right thing bringing this to our attention, boys. What this country needs is more conscientious citizens like yourselves.' He said it so straight-faced I didn't know if he was being a wise guy or not, although I suspected he probably was. If in doubt, I usually suspect someone's being a wise guy.

And then I could hardly believe what he did next. What he did was, he held out his hand. He actually wanted to congratulate us on being such conscientious citizens by shaking our hands. He just held it out over the top of the counter, without bothering to stand up or anything, with his two thumbs pointing at the ceiling. To tell you the truth, I didn't know what to do at that. My first instinct was to get the hell out of there. The thought of those two thumbs clamping down over the top of my own hand made my skin crawl. And I figured they couldn't really shoot me for refusing to shake hands. But then I started to look at the whole situation from a different angle. By now I was almost certain the cop *was* being a wise guy, and that he was just lapping up my obvious discomfort. He definitely knew the effect his proffered two-thumbed hand was having on me. So instead of getting the hell out of there, like I wanted to, what I did was I shook his crummy double-thumbed hand. I took a real good grip and just shook the hell out of it. I think he looked a little disappointed at that. At least, I like to think so.

In any case, I was right. I could still feel my skin crawling when we stepped back into the sunlight.

34

That night I dreamed about the crazy clown again. You'd have thought, under the circumstances, that if I was going to dream about anything I'd have dreamt about giant sea slugs, or knuckle-cracking policemen, or old ladies being swallowed alive, but I didn't. I dreamed about that damn clown.

For some reason he was shooting clay pigeons with an ancient blunderbuss, and just laughing his head off. I don't know what he was laughing about, though, because he was a lousy shot. He couldn't hit the side of a barn, he was such a lousy shot. But he was laughing so hard he actually popped a couple of big yellow buttons off his clown suit, and then his clown face started to melt. Then his real face started to melt. And then he turned into a giant ice-cream cone. And then a dog with Louie Louie's face came along and started to lick it up off the sidewalk. I forget what happened next, but it was still a helluva dream. Even while I was dreaming it, I remember thinking to myself that maybe it wasn't such a bad thing that I couldn't usually remember them, if that's what my subconscious was coming up with. I kind of hoped I wouldn't remember that one as well, but I did. Most of it, anyway. If I could have been bothered, I might even have tried analysing it, but I couldn't be bothered. And then, on top of all that, I woke up to the sound of a goddam rock smashing through my bedroom window.

It gave me a nasty fright. I wasn't a particularly jumpy person, although I can get pretty nervous sometimes, but a rock through my bedroom window first thing in the morning makes me jump every time. It definitely wasn't the most relaxing way to greet a new day. I looked around in a daze, thinking I was under attack or something, that the city was being bombed, and saw my window lying on the floor in pieces. There was also a dirty great rock, the size of a tennis ball, sitting on the carpet. I jumped out of bed and went over to take a look through the hole in the wall where the window used to be.

I should've guessed.

'Louie Louie, you damn maniac! I'm gonna kill you one of these days!'

He was standing in the street below, grinning up at me like a naughty little buddha or something. He'd been breaking my window like this for years now. He'd just throw a rock at my window whenever he couldn't be bothered using the front door. He used rocks like other people use doorbells. I didn't mind that so much, except he was such a lousy judge of rock. He said the little ones never woke me up, and that it was a fine line between what would wake me up, without breaking the window, and what would also wake me up, while breaking it. Incidentally, when I say he looked like a little buddha, I mean it. His whole family did. They were all extremely buddha-like, or buddha-ish. They were pretty cute, when you saw them all together.

'Wuddaya gonna do?' he called back up to me from right in the street, as if it were a perfectly normal place to have a conversation with somebody still in their bedroom. 'Beat me to death with your pecker?' That's when I realised I was standing at the window naked. I sometimes do sleep naked, as a matter of fact. 'I've seen bigger dicks on fleas!'

'Wuddaya smash my window for, you crazy sonuvabitch?' I yelled back, but covering my pecker all the same.

'Wuddaya mean?' *he* yelled back. 'Goddam rock did it, not me.'

That was Louie Louie's logic all over. He was always blaming inanimate objects – golf clubs, pinball machines, rocks, you name it – for something or other. They'd miss putts, tilt, smash windows and just about every other damn thing, but never him.

'Well, wuddaya want anyway?' I asked. 'Wuddajado? Crap in your bed or something?'

Louie Louie grinned up at me and I knew he had something good up his sleeve. When he had something that good, you just knew it. He couldn't hide it if he wanted to. He was a lousy poker player too. We both were.

'Wanna know a secret?' he said, and I knew he had something good up his sleeve for sure. I hated it when he had something that good.

'You're a retard and I'm not?' I suggested.

You might think I'd have tried being a little more civil to him if I wanted to hear whatever it was he had to say, but then you don't know Louie Louie. Being civil is just about the last thing you want to do. If you're civil about it, you'll be there all day. You'll die of old age before he'll tell you what it is he's got up his sleeve if you're civil about it.

'That's funny, Montanna. You really can peel 'em off

any time of the goddam day, can't you? Look at me. I'm laughing my guts out down here. Boy. Still, if you don't want to know, that's fine by me. No skin off my potato. What do I care?' He stuffed his hands in his pockets and pretended to look like he had somewhere else to go. Like, if I wasn't interested in his big secret, then he didn't even give a damn. He'd only come round as a favour anyway. He had plenty of other stuff to do. 'Well, so long, wise guy!' Then he really turned to go. But of course the thing with secrets is, and especially Louie Louie's secrets, nine times out of ten the person who knows one wants to tell it more than the other person wants to hear it. Or even if the other person does want to hear it even more than the first person wants to tell it, all you have to do is pretend you don't. All you have to do is look like you don't give a damn. I'll admit it can be risky, *some*times, depending who you're dealing with. Sometimes it can definitely backfire. But I could read Louie Louie like a comic book. There were thought bubbles right above his head. I knew it was only a matter of a minute, at most, before he burst out from around the corner where he was hiding just begging to tell me. I was right too.

'All *right*, all *right*, already. I'll tell ya,' he said, re-appearing about forty-five seconds later, 'ya don't hafta *beg*!'

35

I threw on some clothes and shimmied down a drain-pipe just outside my smashed window. It was a lot easier for me to shimmy down than it was for Louie Louie to shimmy up, or whatever the opposite to shimmy down is. Also, I'd done it hundreds of times. I was a regular Tom Sawyer when it came to shimmying up and down drainpipes. Besides, if Louie Louie fell and broke his stupid neck, and he actually had something important to tell me, I'd never forgive myself.

'So, what's the big goddam secret?' I asked, the second my feet had hit the ground. This of course was a big mistake. It was quite a tactical error. Especially when I had him exactly where I wanted him. The thing is, though, I already had a feeling I knew what it was about – or rather, *who* – and to tell you the truth, I'd become a bit reckless.

'So,' he said. He was cocky as anything again now. He couldn't have helped notice how quick I'd got the hell down there. 'All of a sudden you want to know, do you? The big smug bastard wants to know what old Louie Louie's got to say, hey? Well, maybe I'm not in the mood to –'

There was nothing else for it. I just started making as if to shimmy on back up that old drainpipe again. I probably wouldn't have done it, though. I wanted to hear what he had to say too much.

'*All right, all right!*' he cried, dragging me back down. Boy, it must really be something for him to want to tell it to me that much. '*Jeez!* You're so impatient. No, *wait!* All right, then, ya crummy sonuvabitch. Listen up.' Then he told me his big goddam secret, right there standing in the street. 'Well, you know that little cutie you were so interested in? The one who told me about you stepping in front of that goddam car? You know, Sunday Daffodil, for Chrissakes?' I did. 'Well, guess what? I only just bumped into her on the street, and she only just asked me where I was going, and when I said I was on my way over here to throw a goddam rock through your window, wuddaya think she said?' What did I think she said? Jesus Christ. I had no idea. Not one. My mind was a total blank. 'She only asked me to say goddam "*Hi*".'

Believe it or not, my stomach actually did a backflip. It really did. I felt it. I never knew they actually did that, even though I'd read about it once or twice in really corny novels. Stomachs are always doing stuff like that in really corny novels. Doing backflips or having butterflies or gut feelings. And hearts are even worse, although they're usually busy pounding and bursting and breaking and fluttering and who knows what else. Anyway, they're both as descriptive as hell. I don't know what writers would do without them. And now mine was doing gymnastics as well, and all because of one little word: 'Hi.' I guess I must have just stood there like I was punch-drunk or something, a dopey, pie-eating grin on my face. I must have looked like a real dummy, because Louie Louie started to smirk all over. I mean it. His ears were smirking. His elbows were smirking. His toes were probably smirking inside their shoes. Not that I begrudged him a little fun. After all, matters of the heart, especially other people's, are pretty comical when you think about it. If you look at them a certain way, even the really tragic cases, they're as funny as hell. In fact, the more tragic they are, the funnier they are. Take Romeo and Juliet, for example. I mean, what a couple of morons. And anyway, who knew? Maybe one day it'd be Louie Louie's turn, the poor sucker.

Still, I probably should have said something, instead of just standing there looking like an idiot, but I didn't. You can't help but look like an idiot sometimes when you just stand somewhere not saying anything. I was like a punch-drunk fighter or somebody just waiting to be knocked stupid. Waiting for my next cauliflower ear. While I should have been ducking and diving all over the ring, at least presenting Louie Louie with a moving target, I just stood there, a big, dumb, sitting duck. I even knew I was about to be knocked silly, but it didn't make any difference.

'Boy, oh boy,' said Louie Louie, smirking and shaking his head in a very superior, sorrowful manner. 'You poor bastard. You sure have got it bad.' It was subtle, I'll say that. I mean, it didn't sound like much, but you really needed to hear the way he said it to appreciate it. I can't describe it, but the thing is, he'd really landed one right on the jaw. He'd really hit the nail on the head. I did have it bad. It was a helluva thing to have happened.

'Why don't you shut your goddam mouth, you goddam fat moron,' I told him, and all he did was just crack up all over the place. This could be extremely frustrating. I mean, you do your best to insult someone and you might as well have not even bothered, for all the good it does. 'Well, what the hell are you laughing at now, you dumb ape? What's so funny?'

Louie Louie took a few moments to try and compose himself. When he'd done it, he looked at me with this very incredulous look on his face. This very superior, incredulous, amused look. 'What the hell do you *think* I'm laughing at?' He was having a terrific time. He generally did, though, he found things so hilarious most of the time. 'You really are amusing as hell, Montanna. Didja know that? You really are. You say the most ticklishly funny things.'

Ticklishly funny things. Boy, I could've socked him when he said that. Except I couldn't because I wanted to hear every last detail of his meeting with Sunday Daffodil. The problem was that instead of pretending I didn't give a damn, like I told you I was so great at doing, I'd done the opposite. What a moron. So instead of socking him right in his big fat cakehole, like I wanted to, I stuck my fist in my pocket, and just swallowed my pride. I really choked it down.

'Okay,' I told him, 'so I'm amusing as hell. I say the most ticklishly funny things. Laugh it up, why don'tcha? Be my guest. Bust a gut even. But when you're all done,' I added, very nonchalantly and all, 'perhaps you'd be so obliging as to inform me of any and all particulars pertaining to this chance encounter. If you wouldn't goddam mind, I mean?' I really laid it on like that to hide what I was really feeling. I sometimes did that.

But I couldn't fool Louie Louie. He still knew how much I wanted to knock his teeth down his throat.

He was used to people wanting to do that, though. But being Louie Louie, he still couldn't resist extracting just that little bit more. Of course, I'd have done exactly the same thing.

'Well, lemme just think a minute,' he said, stroking his chin and gazing into space, like he was pretending to try and dredge it all up. 'I know for a fact she said *some*thing, but what it was exactly suddenly escapes me. Boy! Lemme think a minute . . . Man, I've got a memory like a . . . Hey, wuddaya call those things you drain spaghetti in again?'

That's when I jumped on him. For some reason, I don't know why, my sense of humour returned all of a sudden, so I just jumped on him and we both collapsed on the sidewalk. There wasn't anyone around to see, but I wouldn't have cared if there was. I think I suddenly just felt like horsing around because I'd been so serious and uptight about everything and I just wanted to get it all out of my system. But it really took old Louie Louie by surprise. He wasn't expecting it at all.

'Get the hell offa me, ya crazy lunatic!' he bawled at me, because the way we ended up was I was half sitting on him. He'd actually broken my fall because he'd fallen straight back on his ass and I'd fallen on top of him.

'Boy,' I said, still horsing around. 'You're pretty goddam comfortable. Didja know that? Must be all the stuffing.'

'Ya crazy or something?' he said, once I'd got off him and we'd picked ourselves up. He was all concerned about his pants suddenly, brushing them off with his hand. After tearing a hole in the ones he was wearing the day before, he was really looking after this pair.

'If I knew you were gonna attack me I'd never even've told ya about it in the first place. Geez.' But he was already starting to smile about it. He couldn't stay sore for more than two seconds. 'Besides,' he added, 'I've already told you what the hell happened. Swear to God. I bumped into her. Said I was on my way over here to throw a rock through your window. She said, "Tell him I said hi." That's it. End of story.'

End of story.

'But,' he added, with what I think he thought was a knowing wink, 'it wasn't *what* she said, so much as the way she goddam *said* it.'

36

It was early, but Moriarty's opened early. Opened early and closed late. Poor guy. What a life. Sitting up at the counter with our shakes, we could see him pushing a broom around the floor, banging it about under chairs and tables, scowling at nothing in particular. No one could scowl like Moriarty. He could scowl clear across a room, at the back of someone's head, and they'd still know it. He looked even more beat than usual this morning. Maybe it had been a tougher night than usual. Even after twenty-three years I suppose some nights were tougher than others. His movements were stiff and jerky too, like he was using someone else's body. Like he wasn't used to it. He was beginning to look exactly like what he was. A badly run-down human machine.

When he was finished scowling for a while, he drifted over towards Louie Louie and me, and propped himself up against the counter, looking tired as a second-hand suit. I felt terrible for him, seeing him like that. I wished I could do something. I wished I could take his watch for a while so he could get a little lousy sleep. I felt, I don't know why exactly, like he was on guard or something, watching over things. Like he had been for years. He deserved a break, poor guy. Let someone else do it for a while.

He nodded at us. 'Howzyashakes, boys?' he asked.

I put a little extra into my reply. It was the least I

could do. 'In a class of their own, Mr Moriarty,' I told him. 'But not only that. They're in a *school* of their own. They won't even let other milkshakes through the front *door.*'

He smiled, but I could see he was really beat. He was nearly half dead and he could still bother smiling. Some people wouldn't even smile if their life depended on it, to look at them. Lousy bastards. Louie Louie, meanwhile, was busy trying to suck the bottom out of his glass, so Moriarty asked him if he'd like another.

'Why yes, I feel confident I could accommodate another of your rather excellent beverages, my good man,' Louie Louie told him, which I was pleased to see made old Moriarty chuckle to himself as he went back behind the counter and started fixing it. I guess Louie Louie felt terrible too. We both did.

'Better make that two,' I said, even though I hadn't finished my first one yet, and wasn't even really thirsty.

Moriarty chuckled some more, which made me glad I'd said it. 'You boys certainly can suck down my goddam shakes,' he said.

As Moriarty wasn't in much of a talking mood, and there were a few more customers drifting in anyway, we took our new shakes over to a booth to get a bit more comfortable, and slid in next to a big window overlooking the street. That was another thing about Moriarty's. The booths were so comfortable you could sleep in them, which was kind of ironic. Of course I could sleep just about anywhere, as I've mentioned, but even though the booths were so comfortable, I always made a point never to take a nap in one, no matter how drowsy I was feeling. I would hate for old Moriarty to have glanced over and seen me punching out zees like a real goddam somnambulist or something.

After we'd been sitting there a while, just shooting the bull, Louie Louie said, 'You know, Montanna, you really don't look one hundred per cent in the pink, if you don't mind my saying so.' He didn't work up to it or anything. He just said it. 'As a matter of fact,' he continued, peering at me in a way I didn't entirely like, 'you look particularly *un*pink.'

'*Un*pink?'

'Pallid, in point of fact.' Then he peered at me some more, like I was a curious blob of something or other he couldn't quite identify. He was trying to make it out. 'Actually,' he added, really giving me the benefit of his expert opinion now, 'you look one helluva unhealthy specimen all round, old sport. You really do. No kidding.'

By this time I'd got the goddam picture.

'I get the goddam picture, Louie Louie,' I told him. For some reason it'd really needled me. I was touchy as hell lately. 'So wuddaya want me to do, apologise?'

'Well, don't get sore about it,' he said. 'Wuddaya want *me* to do, say you look like a goddam million bucks?'

We didn't say anything for a while. I hadn't meant to snap at old Louie Louie like that, and I felt bad about it. I didn't know what'd got into me. I was moody as hell. So then, to kind of make up for it, I said, 'You know what I'd do if I *had* a million bucks? I'd fly us both to London, England, first class, and book us into the goddam Ritz. Then what we'd do is we'd go to the theatre every night in a couple of Savile Row tailor-made tuxedos and eat room service and guzzle goddam champagne and be flat busted in a week.'

Old Louie Louie gave a big guffaw at this, and accidentally sucked some shake up his nose, which started him coughing and choking and laughing all at the same time. It was quite disgusting, but it made me feel better.

'You know what, Louie Louie,' I told him, 'you've got the table manners of a gorilla. No kidding. You belong in a zoo or something.'

When he'd finished choking, he just glared at me. He was deadly serious all of a sudden. 'Wuddaya goddam mean,' he demanded, 'I've got the table manners of a gorilla? I *am* a goddam gorilla.' Then he jumped up on the booth seat and started beating his chest with his fists and making gorilla noises. '*Oo, oo, oo, oo, oo!*' he grunted.

'Siddown, for Chrissake!' I told him, laughing. 'Unless you want old Moriarty to come over and knock you outa the park with his baseball bat.'

There were quite a few people in the place by this time, but regulars mostly, so no one took much notice. Except for an older couple who had just walked in off the street. They took one look at Louie Louie and walked straight out again.

'*Oo, oo, oo, oo, oo!*' he grunted some more, really getting into character now. Then he got excited all of a sudden and started pointing out the window beside us. '*Oo, oo, oooo!*' I knew even before I looked, just from the way he said it, that it'd be a girl. Louie Louie was always going ape over girls. I told you before he was sex mad.

Then, still laughing my ass off, I glanced out the window. *POW!*

37

It was embarrassing. It really was. If hearing Louie Louie tell me she'd said 'Hi' had made my stomach do a back-flip, seeing her just outside like that, standing on the sidewalk on the other side of the street, without even expecting it or anything, was enough to give me palpi-tations. And my stomach wasn't doing backflips any more, either. It was all twisted up in knots, like a handful of pizza dough. Hell. I guess I was in love for sure, goddammit. No doubt about it. I was.

I instantly ducked down out of sight, the second I saw her, like a fugitive or something. You'd have thought, to see me, that I was on the lam or something. That I had half the cops in the city on my tail. I almost felt like it, too, I was that nervous. If I was lucky, though, she might not have seen me. For all I knew, she might have been blind as a bat, or at least short-sighted. 'But what if she *has* seen me?' I thought. 'What if she comes inside? What *then*? Jesus Christ! I'll probably have a seizure on the spot, is what then, and she'll get to see me keel over right here on the floor! First she sees me piss my pants, now this!' Meanwhile, Louie Louie was still jumping up and down on his seat, doing jungle impressions through the window. If I could've struck him dead on the spot from where I was cowering I'd have done it.

'*Quit it, you crazy sonuvabitch!*' I hissed at him from

almost under the table now, but Louie Louie just looked down at me like I must've flipped my lid, which wasn't so far from the truth. He couldn't understand my behaviour at all.

'Wuddaya doing under the table?' he asked. 'It's *her*, ya stupid moron dumb ass! The lousy love of your life! Your Juliet! Your East! Sunday Daffodil, for Chrissakes!'

I glared at him in a way I hoped conveyed the fact that I'd have been very pleased to rip his head off if I could've reached it. Death rays shot out of my eyes incinerating him on the spot. But of course Louie Louie, being Louie Louie, didn't even notice. Or maybe he did. Maybe he was just playing matchmaker.

Although I couldn't see anything from my position half wedged beneath the table, I had a feeling she was now standing right outside our window. She was probably no more than a couple of feet away. And then, as if to confirm it, I saw Louie Louie's mouth start moving, forming words, which he spoke out loud, but kind of under his breath, like people do when they're talking to someone through glass.

'Come on in,' he said, gesturing enthusiastically. 'There's somebody here just dying to meet you.'

Her voice came from outside, muffled because of the glass.

'*What?*'

Then Louie Louie – *burst into flames, you bastard, combust!* – actually pointed under the table.

'Under – *here*,' he said, pointing down, 'somebody – who's – just – *dying* – to – *meet* – you!'

I couldn't believe he'd done it. That she was about

to come inside. Jesus Christ, I hadn't even combed my hair. I must've looked like hell.

'Louie Louie,' I growled at him, sliding to the floor on my hands and knees, 'when I get back from the bathroom, I'm gonna *kill* you!'

38

I was sore as hell at Louie Louie, but I was even sorer at myself. I stood in front of a mirror and called myself every kind of name I could think of. I was pretty inventive too. I didn't spare my feelings one bit. I deserved everything I could throw at myself, and more. But the funny thing was, even though I knew I was acting like a real sap, I couldn't do a thing about it. I couldn't, not for a cool million bucks, have just walked out there, like any normal person would have, and said, 'You must be Sunday. Hi, I'm Fielding Montanna. Pleased to meet you.' Well, maybe for a million bucks, but who the hell goes around offering people a million bucks just to talk to a girl? What a world that'd be. But even if they *did*, I'm still not sure I could have done it. Can you imagine that? Refusing a million bucks just to talk to a girl because you were so crazy about her you thought you'd have a seizure or something if you did. Anyway, when I'd finished abusing myself, which actually took quite a long time, I just stood there staring at myself in the mirror for a while. I just stood there, leaning on the sink, glowering away. Boy, was I disgusted with myself. I felt terrible. I really felt depressed. I couldn't remember the last time I'd felt that depressed. But then I noticed something, staring at myself in the mirror like that, which at least took my mind off feeling so lousy. Not only did I *feel* terrible, but I looked it, too.

Louie Louie was right. Unpink, he'd said. Pallid. Unhealthy. Jesus! Un*dead*, more like it. To tell you the truth, I got quite a shock. I'd never seen such an unhealthy specimen in my life. I really looked like hell. Admittedly, mirrors in public bathrooms can make the healthiest-looking person in the world look in dire need of life insurance. They can make anybody who's *not* particularly healthy-looking look like Bela Lugosi or somebody. In fact, if you can possibly avoid looking at yourself in public-bathroom mirrors, I strongly recommend it. But to make matters worse, I had the uncomfortable feeling that this time it wasn't being all that unflattering.

I splashed some cold water on my face and tried to get a grip.

'Montanna,' I said, actually addressing myself in the third person, which is a thing I sometimes do when I've got something very particular to tell myself, 'you're certainly acting in a helluva peculiar manner. You really are. And you look like crap. Jesus, if I didn't know better, I'd think you were crazy high on drugs or something. I would. I'd think you were flipping out. Or flipped. Do you know what I'm talking about? Do you? You do. Well, that's something, I suppose.'

I peered at my crazy Bela Lugosi reflection some more, but I was done giving myself a talking-to. Instead, I kind of started horsing around a bit. 'Good eeevening,' I drawled instead, in my best Transylvanian accent. 'Good eeevening. I vant – to suck – your blood!' I peered right into my own eyeballs, really examining them, which is something else I recommend you avoid. It was actually quite disturbing. I didn't like the look of them at all. They seemed to kind of recede the harder I stared at them, like they were somehow boring their way back-wards through my skull. But at the same time they also seemed to grow brighter the further back they went, until finally they were nothing but fiercely burning pinpricks pulsing at the bottom of their two black sockets.

'Boy, oh boy!' I said out loud. 'Crazy eyes.'

Then I splashed some more water on my face, or at least what I thought was water. Instead, I got a face full of stinking black sludge. I'd left the tap running, and it was spilling out of the faucet, already beginning to clog up the sink. My hands and face were dripping with it. That's when I started cursing again. 'Goddam lousy plumbing!' I said. 'God*dam* it!' But before I could really get into it, I suddenly realised I wasn't alone any more. There was someone else standing right next to me at the next sink and I hadn't even noticed. I figured he must have been in a cubicle, or else just quietly slipped in. Even before I'd got a good look at him, though, I wasn't too crazy about him. I don't know why. And then I noticed something that got my attention right away. He was holding something that looked exactly like the crazy-looking box from the beach, the one we'd left embedded in the sand. Its crazy knobs and wires were sticking out all over the place. I could even hear it gently humming.

I kind of gave the guy a sidelong glance, just to be sure the mirror wasn't playing tricks on me. You can't trust bathroom mirrors. Anyway, he must have noticed, because he giggled. That was it. Just giggled. It was only a quick glance, but it was enough to take in his general appearance. He was dressed in a tattered old tuxedo,

161

very corny and old-fashioned. It looked like velvet, but very worn and shiny. His head, which was enormous and perfectly round, like a beach ball, looked like it had been blown up with a bicycle pump, while his enormous white gloved hands had fingers like sausage balloons. Then he giggled again and hugged his strange contraption, twitching all over.

Man, I thought, he must be *really* crazy high on drugs, and then I turned around to get the hell out of there. But as I did I caught a glimpse of myself in the mirror, my face all mottled with sludge. I looked a mess. So instead I grabbed a handful of paper towels and did my best to make myself a little more presentable. But the tap was still turned on, and the sink was starting to overflow, so I tried to turn it off. I didn't like to think of old Moriarty having to clean it up on top of everything else. But it wouldn't stop. The handle just spun around in my hand. 'Lousy plumbing,' I said again, and turned to go. I'd just have to tell Moriarty on the way out, which was probably all he needed. But as I did, the big-headed freak started twiddling a couple of knobs on his machine, which caused an instantaneous reaction. He looked like he'd just been hit with a thousand volts, but he still wouldn't let go of that crazy box with its crazy knobs and wires. He was holding on to it like his life depended on it or something.

Boy, he really looked like he was in agonies, but he was grinning at the same time, and still shivering and jerking and giggling like a lunatic as I got the hell out of there.

39

Outside, things had gone all to hell. The whole place was like a monkey cage that'd just been rattled. At first I couldn't figure out what could have happened. I'd only been in the bathroom for – well, I didn't know how long I'd been in there, but not that long. Then I saw Sandman lying sprawled in the middle of the floor with his head cracked open like a coconut. He was lying on his back in a puddle of blood, his legs all twisted up beneath him, with a look of what I can only describe as plain dumb incomprehension plastered across his dumb, pimply dial. It looked like whatever it was happened to him, he never got the chance to figure out why it was happening. Poor guy. Poor dumb bastard.

Sandman, I should probably point out, was another Moriarty's regular, and a pretty quiet guy. He was a pretty good guy, too, in his way. In fact, he was just about the last person you'd expect to find lying on the floor with his brains bashed out. I mean, some people's personalities just lend themselves to that sort of thing. If you were to hear they'd just had their brains bashed out, you wouldn't be the least bit surprised. But not old Sandman. He wasn't that kind of guy at all. He just had to have been in the wrong place at the wrong time.

Everybody was trying to get a good look, naturally, but the cops were already on the scene, johnny on the spot, pushing them back. They were determined to spoil everybody's fun, but people were still trying to force their way in through the front door from outside, while the windows were full of ugly, leering, eager faces squashed up against the glass, desperate to see inside. Poor old Sandman. He'd never been so popular.

I found Louie Louie, but there was no sign of Sunday. It was funny, but I was relieved as hell at that. Even after my recent encounter with the big-headed freak in the bathroom, and now poor dead Sandman, lying sprawled on the floor with his brains leaking out, I was relieved because I wouldn't have to talk to her.

'Jesus, Montanna!' said Louie Louie, when he saw me. 'Where've you been? Man, you should've seen it!'

'Seen what? What the hell happened to Sandman?'

The cops were busy herding us out the front door with their batons by this stage, away from the action. Securing the scene. Sandman wasn't going anywhere.

'He just went loco! I've never seen anything like it!' said Louie Louie.

The street outside was all abuzz. Two or three cop cars had pulled up out front, their blue lights flashing, and the cops were busy keeping the crowd back, which continued to swell, everybody eager to join the party. People were craning their necks for a glimpse inside, desperate to see the body, and everyone, as usual, seemed to have an opinion.

'He must've been crazy high on drugs or something!' said someone.

'Did you see it? I saw the whole thing. *Pow!*' said someone else.

'Wuddaya expect, crummy run-down joint like this? Oughta be demolished.'

'Goddam kid probably had it coming!'

'He just went crazy all of a sudden,' explained Louie Louie, calmer now, remembering to breathe, as we watched the cops shove old Moriarty into the back of one of the flashing cop cars. His hands were cuffed behind his back. 'After twenty-three years, can you believe it, he finally dozes off, standing right there leaning up against the counter! No one even goddam noticed! But then someone did, and they nudged someone else, who nudged the next guy, and pretty soon everyone in the place knew it and was just staring like crazy at him, standing there sleeping like a baby. Man, you could've heard a flea fart!'

The cops slammed the door after him, and old Moriarty just sat inside, looking tired as hell, tireder, staring blankly back at the surging crowd all around him. I couldn't believe it. I tried to catch his eye, to somehow let him know – what? I didn't even know what it was I wanted to let him know, but it didn't matter anyway because he didn't see me. How long had he managed to snatch, I wondered. How many precious seconds of oblivion?

'And then old Sandman, who I guess everyone had forgotten to nudge, and who was sitting over in a booth all by himself just minding his own business, starts sucking on his ice-cream float!' Sandman always drank ice-cream floats. He was crazy about them. 'Only thing is he hoovers it all up and starts chasing the dregs round the bottom of his glass with his straw and making a helluva racket about it.'

They switched on the siren and started to drive away. '*Waa, waa, waa, waa, waaaa!*' it said, or something like that.

'And old Moriarty,' continued Louie Louie, as the crowd started to drift away, and the remaining cops sealed up the place like a tomb, 'suddenly wakes up, realises what the hell has happened. He looks around, sees old Sandman still sucking on his straw. Then he reaches under the counter, pulls out a baseball bat, walks over to where old Sandman's sitting, happy as a kid in a candy store, and calmly splits his head open like a ripe melon.'

40

I felt so terrible I went to bed for a couple of days after this. Just to make sure, I knocked myself out and everything. I felt terrible and I was suddenly tired as hell. I hoped the clown wouldn't bother me and he didn't. Nothing did. I could have slept through an earthquake. I could have slept through the end of the world or something. When I did finally wake up, though, I felt unexpectedly happy and refreshed. I felt better than I had in weeks. Months maybe. I really felt good, which is funny, because I don't, generally. I mean, I've never been one of those people who wake up just bursting with energy and enthusiasm. It generally takes me a while to get going. You know, to warm the hell up. Then after waking up so refreshed and everything, I just lay there for a while, hands behind my head, idly turning things over in my mind.

I wondered whether there'd been any news about what had happened. I hadn't forgotten about that. I wondered whether it had been in the papers and everything. I guessed so, but what do they know anyway? Goddam nothing. Some old guy had bashed some kid's brains out and been carted off in the back of a cop car. End of story. There wasn't much else to say on the subject, except that Moriarty's was closed for business, and who the hell cared about that, except a handful of kids? In all my life, Moriarty's had never been closed for more than a few hours each night. In fact, it was probably already boarded the hell up. The cops were probably afraid people would take the opportunity to break in and try and find out whether there was any truth behind all the rumours about labyrinthine libraries and dungeons. Maybe they'd even found a bomb-making factory down there and didn't want to alarm the city. As if it wasn't already alarmed. I didn't like the thought of it being all boarded up, though, and wished I hadn't thought of it. It was like someone had died or something. Of course, someone *had* died, I know, but this was different. Sandman was a nice enough guy and all, in his way, but I wasn't exactly heartbroken about him. I guess I'd miss him, but only like you'd miss a piece of familiar furniture or something. Like a chair you never even sat on. I know that probably sounds bad, but it's the truth. Moriarty's was different, though.

I'd obviously blown it with Sunday, too. She must've thought I was crazy. A real jerk. Louie Louie, once everything had calmed down a bit, and the initial shock had worn off, told me she'd been nice about it and everything – me hiding in the bathroom, I mean – but still. Of course, he didn't *say* I was hiding in the bathroom (at least he said he didn't). What he *said* he said was that I wasn't feeling very well, which was not only pretty tactful (for Louie Louie) but true. Of course, for all I know what he *actually* said was that I wasn't feeling very well because I had a terrible case of diarrhoea and had just crapped in my own pants. That would be just like Louie Louie. He'd think that was hilarious. The thing was, though, although I hoped he didn't *really* say it, it didn't really matter what he'd said. It didn't actually make a bit of difference. I'd blown it no matter what.

Still, like I say, I woke up feeling pretty good, considering. I felt pretty enthusiastic about things, too. In general, I mean. Even if Moriarty's *was* closed, and Moriarty was in some stinking cell somewhere, and Sandman was dead, and I'd blown it with Sunday. I was still looking forward to the day ahead, the week ahead. I actually felt like making plans – not big ones, you understand, not exactly life-changing ones, but plans all the same. There was no reason for it. Well, no concrete reason anyway. I hadn't suddenly decided on the benefits of positive thinking or anything. If anything, I should have still been depressed as hell. But the thing is – and I don't know if you've ever experienced this – I think I just suddenly had one of those 'everything'll be okay' feelings. I mean, I was still sorry about old Sandman, and even sorrier about old Moriarty, who I regarded as a good friend, but that's just the way things go sometimes. Sometimes people bash other people's heads in with baseball bats, and sometimes people get their heads bashed in. I won't go so far as to say it's the natural order of things, but it certainly happens. Actually, maybe that was part of it. Maybe the thought of old Sandman lying there on the floor, and old Moriarty, lying wherever *he* was, in some police cell, staring at some crummy, cracked old ceiling, maybe, made me feel okay by comparison. I wasn't generally a great practitioner of positive thinking. I mean, I guess it works and everything, that it makes the world *seem* a better place, but it's still a crock all the same. Still, I think I realised things could certainly be a whole lot worse after all. Not for Sandman, of course, and probably not even for

Moriarty, but for me. My life really wasn't so bad, all things considered, so why kill yourself about it?

And on that corniest of rosy notes I threw back the covers and positively leapt out of bed. Boy, I sprang out like a kid on Christmas morning! I couldn't wait to see what I'd find under the old tree. And then, before my feet had hardly hit the floor, I saw it, and all that phoney positive claptrap just went flying straight out the window. It flew out the window and took a swan dive straight to the sidewalk below. Splat! Man, it was a helluva sight first thing in the morning.

'*Jeezus goddam Christ!*' I said, and nearly threw up on the spot. My bed was crawling with maggots, big fat sonsuvbitches rolling around with indigestion. '*Jeezus goddam Christ!*' I said again, staring at the mess of them.

I was wearing a pair of old shorts and a T-shirt, and I felt something tumble out from under the shirt and bounce off my foot onto the carpet. I looked down.

Oh man.

I pulled up the shirt, and a bunch more dropped out.

'Oh shit,' I said, and fainted.

41

When I fainted I must've cracked my head on something, because I had a terrific throbbing in it when I woke up. One eye was sticky with blood, too. I could feel a fly paddling round in it. At first, though, after waking up, I wasn't too sure what had happened. My first reaction was I wasn't where I was supposed to be. I didn't exactly know where I *was* supposed to be, but I knew it wasn't lying on my bedroom floor with a sticky eye and a fly paddling round in it. I knew that much, at least.

Once I'd remembered what had happened, though, I guess I must have tried not to think too much, because what happened next is kind of hazy and confused. I definitely wasn't thinking straight, anyway. I guess I tried not to think about it in case I fainted again, or just because it was easier not to. I must have thrown on some clothes, and then managed to slip out of the house unseen. I didn't use the drainpipe this time. I used the door. I remember I was careful as a mouse creeping out, though. All I needed would have been to bump into one of my doting parents. The way I was feeling, that would have just killed me. I couldn't have stood it. I probably would have got a lecture about going out looking like a bum. They probably would have noticed my shoelaces were untied, or my shirt wasn't buttoned up properly. I'm not saying they *were* untied, or it *wasn't* buttoned up properly, you understand. But that's just the kind of thing they'd have noticed if they were. And if it wasn't that, it'd be something else. Anyway, they would have been disappointed as hell, that's for sure – seeing me with my shoes untied and my shirt unbuttoned and my head all busted open and maggots tumbling out all over the place. They'd have thought it was terribly unseemly, leaving the house looking like that. If they even noticed.

The streets were deserted. I don't know what time it was, but I couldn't ever remember seeing them so empty. I thought at first it might have been under lockdown or something, that there must have been another outrage perpetrated while I'd been out cold. Someone or other is always perpetrating some outrage somewhere or other, or else we are. But in that case there'd have been cops and the army and whoever else crawling all over the place. This felt more like the whole city had just decided to relocate during the night. To start again somewhere new, maybe. Move someplace nicer. To leave the city to the rats, and the madmen, and the big-headed freaks. Or maybe it just *felt* deserted. Maybe it was exactly the same as the day before, and the day before that. Maybe nothing had even changed.

Actually, it reminded me of some paintings I'd once seen at the Met or somewhere. I'm crazy about art, although I hardly ever go to museums or galleries. The main reason I don't go is because I feel quite self-conscious looking at paintings in public. I don't mean because it's corny or anything. In fact, just the opposite. Looking at a painting, at least one that I really like, I feel as if I'm naked, especially if I'm really crazy about it. I feel exposed. It's so intimate it's almost indecent, especially in a public place. If the gallery's deserted, that's not so bad, although even then you never know when someone might just walk in and surprise you. I guess I just feel a bit uncomfortable being that naked in front of strangers. Of course, my parents collect it by the square yard. Art, I mean. But it doesn't mean anything to them. They use it like wallpaper or something. I think I've already mentioned how bad their taste is. It stinks. I don't think I could stand it if they ever bought a painting by the guy I'm thinking of, or anyone any good. It just wouldn't be right.

Of course, the guy I'm thinking of's paintings have some pretty dramatic flourishes, like white gloves nailed to walls and old statues striking corny classical poses, usually with an arm missing, or maybe a head. But despite this, they're really very realistic, although kind of strange and unnerving at the same time. Looking at them, although everything is very flat and two-dimensional, you really get the feeling that something's going on in them, even if it's probably impossible to ever know what. If you're not careful, you feel like you might disappear into them and never find your way back. Anyway, the street was so quiet and strange and foreboding even, that that's what it reminded me of, if you've ever seen any of the pictures I'm talking about.

But, like I say, I wasn't thinking very straight. To be honest, I don't know what the hell I was thinking. My recollection of exact events is pretty hazy, but I do know I eventually ended up back at the beach somehow. I know that much. I don't know why I went back there, but I did. Maybe it'd been at the back of my mind. What had happened there. I don't remember getting there

173

either, but again, I guess I did. The city was like a dream. I might have been sleepwalking through it. I remember one thing about getting there, though. I remember I was chased by a dog, or maybe even a pack of them.

I'm usually crazy about dogs. I've never had one or anything, but I'm crazy about them all the same. As a general rule I much prefer them to people. In fact, I can't understand anyone *not* preferring them to people. I mean, what's not to prefer? Of course, some people are always complaining about how bad they smell, which is funny if you've ever been on a crowded subway about five-thirty in the afternoon. Same thing goes for biting. In fact, the only thing I'm *not* so crazy about is the fact they're so crazy about us. It doesn't make too much sense, when you think about it, considering how badly we treat them half the time. As far as I'm concerned, that's their only weak point, though. They can be really lousy judges of character.

But the thing is, as crazy as I am about dogs, I wasn't too crazy about this dog – or pack of them – obviously. I was too busy running like hell. I don't know how far or long they chased me, but by the time I got to the beach, and collapsed in the sand, I'd managed to lose them. Or else maybe they'd just given up. Either way, I was certainly relieved not to have been torn limb from limb, I remember that, which is what I'd been imagining was about to happen every second. Then, once I'd lost them, or once they'd given up, I just lay there, on my back in the sand, amongst all the junk and debris and stinking piles of garbage, staring up at the big old sky, trying to gulp down what felt like solid lumps of air.

After a while, once the lumps weren't quite so big any

more, and I could swallow them without too much trouble, I sat up and looked around. Until then I hardly even knew where I was. I could have been anywhere. But it was the same old beach, same old slick, shining sea. Looking at it, it could have been the same day even. Then for a moment I wasn't entirely sure it wasn't. It's pretty hard to tell sometimes. Except beside me I felt a Louie Louie-shaped void. There was a hole where he wasn't. It was like I was part of a nearly completed jigsaw puzzle, but the Louie Louie-shaped piece was missing. Then I started to imagine the world, and everything in it, as a great big jigsaw puzzle too, with everything and everyone a separate piece of the puzzle. But of course it could never make any damn sense, because for one thing you were just another piece, and for another, just when you thought you could maybe see the big picture, even though you *were* just a tiny, insignificant part of it, you realised there *was* no big picture. It didn't exist. There was just a million billion tiny insignificant pieces of other people's puzzles. And then, because my head was beginning to buzz gently, I just stared a while at that slick, shiny soup, lap-lap-lapping at the shore, like it was slowly trying to gnaw it away, grain by grain, and tried not to think about what was under my shirt.

Take it from me, that kind of thing isn't so easy to ignore. The more I tried not to think of it, the less I could think of anything else. Anything at all. And I really tried. I searched my mind, calmly at first, methodically even, looking for something, anything, to latch on to, something that would stick, but nothing would. Nothing would take purchase. The fact of it was all there was. It was sheer and shapeless and smooth and filled my head. There wasn't any room for anything else. And the more I searched, the more frantic I became, until finally, out of desperation to take my mind off trying not to think about it, I started thinking, without even meaning to, about that crazy old lady with her pram full of crazy eyeless dolls, the one who never saw coming whatever the hell it was she never saw coming, and what it was she'd been about to say.

For some reason that had really come to bug the hell out of me.

Of course, I'd already figured I'd never really know, and it's not letting you in on any big secret to tell you I was right. I never would know, but that's just the way it goes, I guess. Whatever it was she'd been about to tell us, Louie Louie and me, we were just going to have to get along without it. I guess people don't get to say certain things just about every day of the week, and just as many people don't get to hear what those people don't get to say. And maybe it doesn't make any difference anyway.

But then again, I couldn't help thinking, maybe it does.

Maybe what that old lady had to say was so important someone, or something, *some*where, was so determined to stop her saying it that they created that stinking sea monster just so that it would leap out of the sludge at that exact moment right on top of her. Maybe what she had to say was the key to something or other maybe better left locked. Better left unsaid. Of course, by the time my thoughts had got to this point, I realised I was sounding crazier than old Crazy Cazayly, who was so crazy he finally started to make sense and was locked up, lickety-split, before whatever he had to say had time to spread. But at least it had taken my mind off what was under my shirt, and the shapeless fact of it still lurking somewhere in my head, just waiting to sneak back.

And then, after realising I was sounding as crazy as old Crazy Cazayly, I don't know why, but I started thinking about one time when I was just a kid, and I stepped on this nail sticking up through an old plank of wood. I wasn't wearing any shoes, and I remember looking down at the point of the nail where it had come right through the top of my foot, and feeling surprised that something could actually go right through, just like that. I remember being surprised as hell at that. I guess I hadn't realised how soft I was. But the thing is, we are. Soft, I mean. All of us. That every day we aren't splattered to bits is a miracle.

And that was just about when I noticed it. A small figure in the distance, standing at the very edge of the headland jutting up at the end of the beach.

Of course, I was too far away. I shouldn't have been able to see who it was, at that distance, but I could. It was like I suddenly had telescopic vision or something, or maybe an up-to-now-unknown zoom function. I was a camera all of a sudden.

Naturally it was her.

Sunday Daffodil, I mean.

I guess I should have been pretty surprised, seeing her there like that, but I really wasn't. I wasn't surprised at all. But it wasn't like I'd been expecting her or anything, either. It wasn't one thing or the other. It wasn't anything. I guess she was just another part of

177

the puzzle. Another tiny, insignificant piece that didn't make much difference maybe to anything but me. I guess she fitted, is what I'm trying to say. There was a space up there on the cliff for her and she slotted right into it. Nice and neat. Nothing else would have, I guess. The picture was gradually coming together, but it would still never be a picture *of* anything. Of course I didn't understand any of this at the time. There was nothing *to* understand.

I sat watching her, as she stood there, with my telescopic eyes and everything. She was teetering right on the edge, staring up at the sky, the cliff face dangling at her feet. She was only about two inches from the edge. I hadn't really thought about it before, but she was so intent on it, the sky I mean, so hard and bright and brittle as glass, and just as likely to crack, that I looked up at it as well.

It certainly was beautiful.

I guess it was just about the most beautiful sky I'd ever seen. Which, funnily enough, was Sunday's exact same thought as she took a step forward over the edge.

42

She didn't make a sound. Not until she hit the ground, at least. A soft body slamming against rock. Of course I'd heard my own body slam against metal, or rather, metal slam against it. But this was different. Gravity can be an ugly, sickening thing. Her body made an ugly, sickening sound as it slammed against the rocks below. But before she'd even landed I was on my feet, sprinting towards her. I thought I could catch her in my arms. I stretched them out, impossibly, to try and catch her. Of course, I shouldn't even have been able to hear her hit the rocks, at that distance, but I could.

SLAP!

My ears, like my eyes, had grown suddenly, somehow, impossibly keen. Although of course she didn't really make a slapping noise. I can't describe the noise she really made, and even if I could, I wouldn't do it.

And then what happened was, she didn't move. This wasn't so very surprising, I know, but in another way it was. In another way it was the most astonishing thing in the world. One minute she was standing at the edge of the cliff looking up at the sky and the next she was just lying there in a crumpled, shapeless heap. She'd changed shape, in a second, shaking off her old one, becoming shapeless. The ground had taken away what she'd been and left nothing in its place.

I ran towards her. I was still running when an enormous

black bird suddenly dropped out of the sky and landed beside her crumpled, shapeless body. It was the biggest, ugliest bird I'd ever seen in my life. It was huge, prehistoric almost.

I picked up a stone as I ran and hurled it at the goddam monster, which gurgled and croaked like it had a craw full of mud. Then it flapped its great reeking wings and lifted up off the rocks a few feet, before dropping down again and sinking its talons in. With another flap it rose up into the air, clutching Sunday beneath it, and I picked up another rock and threw it as hard as I goddam could, while I screamed at it like a goddam madman sonuvabitch.

43

It dropped her directly above me, from about twenty feet, and I heard my leg snap as I caught her in my arms. Boy, that was all I needed. I needed a broken leg like old Sandman needed another hole in the head. But the thing was, I'd caught her. I had her. She'd fallen through the air in slow motion. I guess that's how I managed to catch her. 'I've got you, I've got you,' I repeated, not taking my eyes off her as she tumbled through the air towards me. It was funny, but suddenly I had all the time in the world. I might have been waiting for a bus or something. Then my leg snapped in slow motion too. I felt it bend and snap and the bone stab right through the skin. But there wasn't any pain. I didn't feel a thing. I mean, I felt it, but I didn't. Then everything sped up again and we collapsed in another shapeless, crumpled heap. Just like that. I guess gravity had caught up with us again, but I had her. That was the thing. I held her tight, cradling her broken body in my arms, the great black bird hovering above us, suddenly blocking out the sun. Then I looked down into her face and she suddenly opened her eyes.

BAM!

'Hi,' she said, smiling up at me.

Boy, I liked that smile. I really did. I can't explain how *much* I liked it. I'd *like* to, but I just can't. It's impossible. Then after saying 'Hi' she tried to sit up in my arms but she couldn't. Her head just lolled on the end of her cracked neck like a crazy rag doll's, and looking down I could see the bone sticking out through my own leg. I guess I should have swooned or something, seeing something like that, but I didn't, not yet. At first, though, I hardly knew what to say, but then I did.

'I guess you must be Sunday Daffodil,' I said, quite suavely I think, although I'm not exactly the greatest judge in the world of that sort of thing. Also, my head was beginning to swim quite badly. 'Well, hi. I'm Fielding Montanna.'

It probably wasn't even the least bit suave in reality, but I like to think it was even if it wasn't. Suaveness can be an extremely difficult thing to pull off successfully. It really can.

She smiled again and I noticed there were pale scars on her wrists where they hung limply at her sides.

'Very pleased to finally make your acquaintance, Fielding Montanna,' she said.

But then, maybe because I was so happy, I thought of something that made me quite nervous all of a sudden, and I had to ask, even if she thought I was crazy.

'Are you real?'

She didn't laugh, or even look at me strangely, like she thought I *was* crazy, like I thought she would. Instead she said, 'Are you?'

'I don't know.' I almost didn't either.

'Tell you what,' she said. 'If you'll believe in me I'll believe in you.'

Then the big black bird dropped out of the sky, and we sank beneath its outstretched wings.

44

After that big black bird dropped out of the sky I didn't remember a thing, not until I opened my eyes and found myself looking at an unfamiliar ceiling from an unfamiliar bed, tucked up like a little kid again. It was a high ceiling, but even though it was so high, I could still see it was all stained and bulging in places. It was really in a terrible condition. I don't know what I mean exactly, but it looked kind of cancerous. It looked diseased or something. It was yellow and stained and bulging in places and all cancerous-looking and just crummy as hell. It was the kind of ceiling that, if you had to stare at it too long, wouldn't do you any good at all. But the room itself, although it wasn't exactly inviting, was strangely familiar. I was sure I'd seen it before somewhere. I couldn't think where, though.

At first I was so fascinated by that incredibly crummy ceiling, and then by the room itself, and where I might have seen it, that I didn't even notice I had company. When I did notice, though, I wasn't even particularly surprised to see who it was, except maybe that there were two of them.

Big-headed freaks, I mean.

They were dressed identically, in tattered tuxedos, the same as the big-headed freak from old Moriarty's bathroom, and they were sitting either side of me, both clutching identical boxes, all knobs and wires, happily giving themselves soundless electric shocks. These boxes, as far as I could tell, were the same as the one from Moriarty's bathroom and the one from the beach that'd been buried in the sand. In fact, there wasn't a single thing to tell one big-headed freak or his crazy contraption from another. For all I knew, they might have been twins, or maybe even triplets, and even then it crossed my mind to wonder just how many more of them there might be.

They continued giving themselves these tremendous electric shocks, grinning and shuddering and squirming with every jolt, their fat sausage fingers frantically working the controls. You'd have thought they'd have been quite clumsy with those big, fat, sausage fingers of theirs, but they weren't. They were very dexterous. They were really enjoying themselves, too, if that's the right word. They were having such a good time they didn't pay me any attention at all. I might have been invisible or something. I might not even have been there. When they *did* finally notice me, though, noticed that I was awake maybe, they stopped what they were doing and just sat there, watching me. They didn't say anything, they just sat there twitching and grinning at me like I was some newborn baby or something, or a dog about to do a trick.

There was a soft humming buzz, but it might have been in my head.

I tried to speak, and realised my lungs were empty. They'd collapsed.

'I can't – *breathe*.'

One of them leaned over and patted my arm, like a regular Florence Nightingale or somebody. He was as concerned as hell all of a sudden. It was touching almost. It really was.

'Relax,' he squeaked, in a voice filled with helium. He had the highest voice I'd ever heard. 'There's no need.'

Then he smiled like a real sympathetic sonuvabitch, which might have been more reassuring if his smile hadn't been busy revolving around his big, bulbous moon face. In fact, all his features seemed to have come unstuck, become fluid, like they'd lost the ability to form a face.

I looked at the other one. His mouth was somewhere around where his ear ought to have been. 'You're already dead,' it said.

The humming was louder now, and I tried to order my brain to quit it.

'Flies,' I said. 'It sounds like goddam flies.'

The sound was nearly deafening now, more a roar than a humming, and that crummy, cancerous ceiling appeared to be moving somehow. It had changed colour too. It wasn't yellow any more, but black. It was black and alive and crawling. I dragged my eyes away and looked down along the bed.

Oh man.

The blanket was moving too.

Of course I tried not to think of it. I tried like crazy not to think about what was under that blanket, but it was no use. Like I said before, that kind of thing isn't so easy to ignore. I tried to think of *any*thing, in fact, not to think of it, but my head was already so full of it there was no room for anything else. It was already so full up with whatever the hell was under that lousy blanket that there wasn't a thing I could do about it. The fact of it was all there was now. There was nothing else.

Then one of the big-headed freaks, not Florence Nightingale this time, but the other one, leaned forward. Not to pat my arm or whisper words of reassurance, but to grip the top of the blanket with his Mickey Mouse fist. He was balancing his quietly thrumming machine on his lap with one hand, and gripping the top of the blanket with the other. Then he smiled at me from somewhere around the middle of his forehead, and I just knew what he was going to do. In all my life I'd never wanted someone not to do something as much as I wanted him not to do that, but I knew he was going to do it all the same. He was going to enjoy it, too.

I screamed at him not to, or tried to, but he threw it back anyway, the big-headed sonuvabitch, and I looked down to see ten thousand flies stuck to what used to be my body. I was encased in a living, writhing, gorging suit of them. A suit of flies. A fly suit. Then they lifted into the air like a cloud, filling the room, the noise of them like ten thousand needles in my brain.

And there she was at the foot of the bed, her head still lolling at a crazy angle. Her mouth was full of flies.

My two bedside companions thought this, or something, was just goddam hilarious, and started howling hysterically. Maybe it was the look on my face. Maybe it was the look on hers. I guess it's funny what can set a person off. Just about anything can do it. It's also pretty funny what people can look like when they really start up. I mean, if you didn't know what laughing was, and you'd never seen anyone do it before, it'd probably scare the hell out of you the first time you did see it. You'd probably think the person was having some kind of fit or something, or maybe preparing to take a bite out of your neck. Probably the last thing that'd occur to you was that they were having a good time.

Maybe that was how I'd looked to my mother and father the day at the hospital when the doctor told them I'd had a lucky escape and I thought it was so funny I guffawed right out loud. Perhaps I'd looked like I was having a fit, or was preparing to rip their throats out. At the time I thought they'd missed the joke, but maybe there hadn't been any joke to get.

The two big-headed freaks continued to look like they were having a fit, or else preparing to rip our throats out. They howled hysterically like people sometimes do when they've forgotten what it is they're even laughing about. But even so, they were only laughing from the neck up. Only their crazy, mixed-up features appeared to be in on the joke. Below that their bodies were still shuddering and twitching and convulsing with the sound-less electric shocks they continued giving themselves. They were still clutching their crummy machines, all knobs and wires, their fat sausage fingers working madly at the controls.

Sunday still hadn't moved.

I called her name, or tried to, over the sound of the howling and the flies, but the word came out a grotesque, feeble croak. '*Sunday!*' She didn't move, sprawled where she was across the foot of the bed in a twisted, inert lump. She was in a pretty bad way, but even then, like that, I'm not kidding, she looked adorable. You should have seen her. Of course, you probably wouldn't have thought so. It probably would've turned your stomach. But she was, all the same. Adorable, I mean. I tried calling her name again. '*Sunday!*' I croaked. 'My sweet, beautiful, broken-necked flower.' I said it like some kind of corny incantation or something, designed to tug at the heart strings of the dead, to bring them back again. And believe it or not, it worked. She blinked suddenly, dislodging the flies that'd been glued to her blank, staring eyes. She tried to raise her head, but couldn't, smiled, and began to retch, coughing up black blood and more flies.

The two big-headed freaks thought this was just hilarious as well. They were already laughing their heads off, of course, but I think this might actually have reminded them of what they'd found so funny in the first place, which now they'd remembered it, they seemed to find twice as funny the second time around. They certainly did have a terrific sense of humour, that's for sure. They had such a terrific sense of humour, the pair of them, that I'd have quite happily broken their necks for them free of charge.

And then, as if the flies and the howling and just lying there unable to even talk tough weren't bad enough, from behind the curtains, goddam it, a hand, a horribly gnarled old hand, suddenly appeared. I wasn't even surprised to see it had two thumbs. I should probably point out here that one wall was almost entirely covered with a very heavy velvet curtain hanging all the way to the floor. It was a very deep burgundy colour, I guess you'd call it, and the hand – or rather, claw – looked terrifically pale against it as it gripped its edge and started to draw it back along its rail. Whoever or whatever it was drew it back very slowly, managing at the same time to remain hidden behind it, presumably shuffling along with it, so that I never got to see any more of whoever or whatever it was than that two-thumbed claw. And as it was drawn back, it revealed a set of French windows behind, straight out of some drawing-room comedy or something. The kind of drawing-room comedy where somebody'd be forever bursting through them with a cry of 'Anyone for goddam tennis?' all goddam day.

But no one did, of course, and no one would be anytime soon, either.

Outside there was a black, inky tide lapping at the glass.

45

That was about when I noticed the monkey.

At first I thought it was a little girl with pigtails, but it was only wearing a cheap, plastic, little-girl mask. It might have been Judy Garland, or maybe Shirley Temple, and was held on by a thin elastic strap. I could see it was only a mask because I could see its monkey eyes through the eyeholes.

It was sitting slumped in a corner, like maybe it was dead or something. Except I could see straight away that it wasn't because of its eyes, which I could see through the eyeholes, and which were watching me, and never blinked. Once I could see that it was a monkey, I wondered how I could ever have mistaken it for a little girl, even with the mask. But then, the more I watched it watching me, the less sure I became that it *wasn't* a little girl after all, or at least a monkey with a little girl's face. A monkey with a little girl's face with monkey eyes.

I don't know how long we watched each other like that, but however long it was, it felt longer. I don't know whether you've ever tried watching someone watching you without letting them know that you were watching them and pretending you didn't even know you were being watched in the first place, but it's about as difficult as it sounds. For some reason, though, now that I'd seen it, I really didn't want to take my eyes off it. I didn't trust it one goddam bit. In fact, I trusted it about half as far as I'd like to have kicked it, even though as a rule I'd never actually kick an animal. I guess there was just something about big-headed freaks and little-girl-mask-wearing monkeys that brought out my violent side. And it wasn't as if the monkey had even done anything, except just sit there like it was dead. It hadn't even let out so much as a peep. But I still didn't trust it enough to take my eyes off it, only I did, without even meaning to, when Sunday suddenly started retching again at the foot of the bed. In an instant the monkey had leapt to its feet, as if activated by some silent, prearranged signal or something. Maybe it had been waiting for me to look away the whole time. Anyway, before I knew it, not only had it leapt to its feet, but it was busy cranking up an ancient gramophone player that, just like it, I hadn't even noticed before. It was strange that I hadn't, too, because it was identical to the one I used to play my old records on until my parents dumped them all in the trash that time. It had a big old elegant ear trumpet, big enough to fit a person's head, and was really a very handsome machine. I wondered whether the monkey was going to play some jazz. Something elegant as hell, to fit the mood. But then the needle bit deep into a record, and a crackly 'Blue Danube', that beautiful, corny, crazy old waltz, joined the howling, buzzing cacophony.

The two big-headed freaks immediately jumped up out of their seats, almost as if they'd been ejected, and dragged us, Sunday and me, without so much as a 'By your leave' or a 'May I please have this dance?' out of bed and onto the floor. To tell you the truth, I was pretty surprised they could drag themselves away from their machines, which they left humming softly on the bed, but they were suddenly like a couple of sailors on shore leave. Except I never heard of a couple of sailors on shore leave dancing to that mad old waltz. And they were pretty good dancers, too, like a couple of nightmarish, big-headed Fred Astaires. But that didn't necessarily make us Ginger Rogers, doing everything they did, only backwards. We were more like a couple of broken rag dolls instead. But they danced us round and round all the same, as elegant as hell, still howling like madmen, while the monkey shrieked and screamed and did backflips on the bed.

And suddenly, in my mind's eye, and all over the country, I could see people dancing in the streets. Hundreds and thousands of them. Millions even. Old people and young people and middle-aged people and little kids. Businessmen and shopkeepers and workmen and housewives. Crazy people and sane people and people who might have been crazy or sane. Whole blocks, and towns, and cities. They were dancing to the same crackly waltz, that same beautiful, corny, crazy 'Blue Danube'. And everyone was just as elegant as hell. And maybe they were dancing to it all over the world as well, leaping out of beds, and bathtubs, and from behind desks and counters, but I couldn't see that far. But they probably were. Why not? And it oozed from the screens on every street corner, from every television set and radio, growing louder and louder, until people would feel a trickle at their ears, and putting a hand up to feel it, find it wet. Then they'd stare at the tips of their fingers and laugh. 'Blood!' they'd cry, goddam delighted. 'Real blood!' And then they'd carry on dancing all the same, moving closer and closer towards the edge, the edge of buildings, the edge of cliffs.

Man, all over the country people were happily waltzing off buildings and over cliffs. The bodies were piling up like broken toothpicks.

And then the bookcase, which was opposite the bed, began to groan and tremble, before beginning to swing away from the wall, slowly, painfully, like flesh being peeled off bone, an inch at a time. Beyond it, up a few well-worn steps, was a hard, stone passageway. It was suffused with a soft, pulsing, orange glow.

And round and round we danced.

46

It was a swell party, that's for sure. A swell party in hell, or somewhere like it. That is, right up until the moment Louie Louie – good old Louie Louie! – goddam gatecrashed it. Boy, did he make an entrance. Bursting through the door with an Uzi and a cry of '*Die*, you crazy bastards, *die*!' he really let 'em have it. Man, you should have seen him spray that room. It was a whole new side of him I'd never seen before. Of course, I'd never seen him with an automatic weapon before, either. Automatic weapons can bring out a whole new side in just about anyone, I guess. Anyway, the two big-headed freaks were as surprised as hell. I guess they hadn't been expecting company. One minute they were twirling us round and round the floor, having a goddam gorgeous time, and the next they were each doing a brief spastic dance before their bullet-riddled bodies were slapped against the back wall and they slumped in heaps. The monkey had stopped shrieking and turning somersaults and lay on the bed, whimpering.

And the inky black tide rushed in.

47

Of course, Sunday and I didn't entirely escape the ferocious hail of lead, but by this time we hardly even noticed. We were already a couple of wrecks. You should have seen us. Sunday lay where she'd fallen, half propped up against the end of the bed, her head swivelling round on its broken neck, spitting flies and oozing blood. She'd taken a couple of dozen hits, as had I, but we both just looked at one another and burst out laughing. We started laughing our heads off. The room was awash with putrid black sludge from where it was still pouring in through the shattered French windows, and thick with flies and corpses, and we laughed so hard we nearly wet our pants.

'What's so goddam funny?' Louie Louie asked, grinning all over his big fat face from all his heroics. 'Hey, what's so funny?'

At first we were laughing so hard we couldn't even reply. And every time we looked at one another, we laughed even harder. I guess you probably had to be there to really appreciate it, though. For example, Sunday had a bullet hole right between her eyes, which for some reason I found quite hilarious. I wouldn't ordinarily find a bullet hole in somebody's forehead particularly amusing, I don't think, but I did then. I think it was so funny because it was so perfectly dead centre. It was a very nice piece of shooting, even though it was entirely accidental. Also, a piece of the side of my skull had been shot clean off. I could already feel the flies swarming over the soft, oozing wound, sealing it over.

'Louie Louie,' I said to him, 'you're a helluva shot.'

He was, too. He'd managed to hit almost every damn thing in the room, apart from himself. He was probably lucky there hadn't been anything to ricochet off, otherwise he might have cut himself to pieces too, the amount of rounds he let off. Even the big-headed freaks' crazy boxes had been shot to hell. They were still sitting on the bed, fizzing and crackling and leaking sticky pus.

Now he just grinned some more and twirled his Uzi on the end of his trigger finger like a real-life Hollywood cowboy. Like Roy Rogers or somebody. Or Shane. I was just waiting for him to shoot his own goddam foot off next.

'Darn tootin!' he said, before depositing the Uzi with a particularly deft flick of the wrist into a special holster he was wearing, hung low on his hip, like a gunslinger. It suited him, too. He looked good. Very Wild West. 'So, I see you two crazy kids finally caught up with one another. What happened, Montanna? Get sick of hiding out in bathrooms with a dose of diarrhoea?'

He tipped Sunday the old wink, and I strongly suspected by the way she half stifled a smile that that was probably what he *had* told her after all that day at Moriarty's when I *did* hide in the bathroom, but *not* with diarrhoea. I shot him a warning glance, or rather, a warning glare, and growled, half under my breath, 'Louie Louie, I swear, not even Miss Cuthbert'll be able to save your crummy neck this time.'

Miss Cuthbert, you might remember, was the teacher

who broke up our fight when we were five years old. '*What?*' he protested, all wide-eyed innocence. 'What have I done now?' He should have been an actor. He really should. He'd have been perfect at playing all those kinds of guys who wind up in court accused of some crime or other, and even when there's a mountain of incriminating evidence against them, and maybe even one or two eyewitnesses thrown in for good measure, they're so convincing at acting all innocent that the jury or whoever still believe they didn't do it, whatever it was, and acquit. 'And wuddaya mean, anyway – save *my* crummy neck?' We must have had this conversation a million times. I'm not kidding. 'If that old Miss Cuthbert hadn't stepped in when she did, Montanna, I'd have murdered you! Everybody said so.'

'You're hallucinating,' I told him. 'You were on the goddam ropes. You were down for the count. If Miss Cuthbert hadn't stopped me, I'd have cut you to ribbons. You'd have been disfigured for life – *more* disfigured for life! They'd have had to send you home in a lunch box.' You should have heard us. We were five years old, for Chrissake. You'd have thought it happened two days ago or something.

Sunday gave a little cough, not coughing up flies or blood this time, but to get our attention. We'd both half forgotten about her. She was still sitting slumped up against the end of the bed, where she'd fallen, although she'd slipped dangerously low into the sludge, which must have been over a foot deep by now, and was still pouring in.

'Sorry to interrupt,' she said. 'But would someone mind shifting my head about two inches to the left? I'd really hate to drown before finding out for sure who would've cut who to ribbons.' Although she said it in a very sarcastic way, she also said it very sweetly and amusingly too. I really liked the way she said things. I'd never realised before that girls could be so sarcastic and sweet at the same time. And funny. She was the most sarcastic, sweet, funny girl I'd ever met. She really was. Boy, was I crazy about her.

But she had a point, too. The way that old sludge was pouring in through the French windows, she'd have been blowing bubbles before too long. It was already lapping at the edge of the passageway behind the bookcase, where the orange glow was still pulsing, stronger and brighter than ever. Or else closer. Also, the flies had regrouped ten deep on the ceiling, and were just starting to swirl overhead in an angry, buzzing blizzard.

'Time to go, I think,' said Louie Louie. Then he just grinned like a real sonuvabitch and produced a big balloon tied to a piece of string from behind his back.

'From the clown,' he said, and handed it to me.

48

We stepped off the window ledge like we were stepping through a door. Of course, I'm not that crazy that I'd normally trust two people's weight to a balloon, even a crazy clown's balloon, but my broken-necked baby was as light and limp as a dead bird, and besides, I had a feeling somehow that it'd be all right. It was still strange, though, just stepping out into thin air. I think in a situation like that, there are thousands of years of evolution telling you not to do it. The same as jumping out of a plane or something. Or blowing yourself up. It just goes against the grain. No other kind of animal would do it, that's for sure. Jump out of a plane, or blow itself up, or step off a window ledge into thin air. It'd never occur to it, for one thing, and even if it did, it'd still never do it. I guess we only do because we think we know what'll happen, even if we don't. That makes all the difference.

Even so, just kind of bobbing there, in mid-air like that, holding on to the balloon with one hand and my other arm around Sunday, I couldn't help looking down and wondering how the ground had got so far away. We must've been a hundred feet up. I probably should have been terrified. I wasn't, though. I just looked back at old Louie Louie, who was standing at the window with his thumbs stuck in his belt, his trusty Uzi hanging at his side. I guess he must have parked Trigger outside in the hall or something.

'Say, Louie Louie,' I said, still bobbing there on the spot, a few feet from the ledge. 'Before you ride off into the sunset, how do we make this thing move?' I meant the balloon. I couldn't see any controls or anything, and wondered whether it might be wish-propelled or something, and all I'd have to do is think of where I wanted to be, and I'd be there.

But Louie Louie just grinned. By the look on his face I could tell he was glad I'd asked.

'Gas,' he said.

I sure would miss that sophisticated sense of humour. It was classic drawing-room comedy, it really was. Old Oscar Wilde would've gone ten rounds with the Marquess of Queensberry for material like that.

'Louie Louie,' I told him, 'you're a goddam riot, kid. Have I ever told you that?'

He gave a very theatrical bow, and we started to drift away.

'Why, thankee, sir,' he said, and I just knew he had one last wisecrack up his sleeve. He'd probably been saving it up this whole time. He gave us this very sweet smile, and suddenly he looked like an overstuffed cupid. Instead of an Uzi, all he needed was a tiny bow and arrow and some wings. 'And may I just say what a goddam handsome couple you make,' he said. 'No kidding.'

49

And so we drifted, floating high above all my old familiar haunts, where just about everything that had ever happened to me, happened. The city was spread out below us like a map, like an open diary of my life. Everything I'd ever done or said or even thought about was done or said or thought about down there, just about. Every dumb, stupid, idiotic thing. I could read it like a book. I could even read between the lines. I even knew how it was going to end, goddam it, or thought I did. Except that now an inky black sludge filled the streets, lapping at doors and windows, seeping through cracks. It was burbling up through drains and gutters, oozing out of fire hydrants and drinking fountains, unstoppable and rank.

People were actually being carried along by it, clinging to whatever they could find to keep afloat. Sofa cushions and soda crates. Deckchairs and garbage cans and whatever else they could find. I even saw one woman hanging on to an open empty suitcase, except it wasn't quite empty, because it had a baby in it. I don't know if it was *her* baby, or whether she'd just grabbed hold of a suitcase which just happened to have a baby in it. It was difficult to tell at that height. Either way, it reminded me of old Moses and the bulrushes, if you've ever heard that old story. The one where baby Moses floats down the Nile, not in a suitcase, of course, but in a basket or something. The Bible's full of stuff like that. I read it a few years back, from cover to cover – both books. The only reason I did was because I was feeling particularly depressed at the time, and this kid from school, Seymour Papert, who was very quiet and shy and who I'd probably never even said two words to in my entire life, gave me this book the size of a brick. I don't know how he knew I was depressed, or why he'd even care, but for some reason he did, and so he gave me this book the size of a brick, and so I read it. I'm a pretty fast reader, when I can be bothered, but I've got lousy taste. Usually when I've finished reading a book I wish I hadn't even read it. Except for the occasional book. The occasional book I'll be crazy about, and will read it about fifty times, like old *Huckleberry Finn*, for example. But not this time. This time, I was *glad* I'd read it. In fact, I wished I'd read it *years* ago. And also, by the time I'd finished it, I wasn't even the least bit depressed any more. In fact, by the end of it, by the time I got to Revelations, with all that fire and brimstone raining down all over the place and everybody being judged, I couldn't even remember what I'd been depressed about. It was a real eye-opener, that's for sure. It certainly did put things into perspective. I mean, by the time I'd got to the end of it, I thought, if people can be stupid enough to believe this old crock – to have believed it for two thousand *years* – then I guess they're just about stupid enough to believe anything. And once you realise that, that people are stupid enough to believe just about anything, then a helluva lot of things start to make a lot more sense. You suddenly realise a lot of the things that we do – the really bad things especially, but everyday things, too – are done because of that. Because as a species we're so goddam dumb. Dumb enough to believe we can do whatever the hell we want. Dumb enough to believe what the government or some crummy old book tells us to believe. Dumb enough to believe that we're any more important than any other poor dumb animal on the planet. And if we can be that dumb – that plain ignorant – then what we really deserve, what we *need*, is pity. And once you realise *that*, you start to look at people and the world in a whole different way. It still might not make much sense, but at least you know it's not meant to. It never did and it never can, which may not sound like much of a consolation, but it's something all the same. Maybe enough, even.

Not, perhaps, for all those people being carried along by that burbling, oozing, inky, black sludge, rising higher and higher all the time. Or for the woman clinging to the suitcase with the baby in it, who might or might not have been its mother, and who suddenly lost her grip, left behind while the suitcase floated free. Or the others, either, inside, doors locked and bolted, hurrying upstairs, arms full of useless valuables, the tide licking at their heels.

But it was enough for me. Enough for me, floating high above the city, taking my whole little world in at a glance, to want to take it in my arms, to hold it and comfort it and whisper those reassuring words I'd imagined someone whispering to me in the ambulance on the way to the hospital, that everything was going to be just fine, it'd see, and to even let it in on the big goddam secret, which was only that there isn't one. The world was laid out below me like a jigsaw puzzle, now nearly complete, but still not a picture *of* anything. How could it be? It was, after all, at the end of the day, at the end of *days* even, just a puzzle. Nothing more. There wasn't really a picture to piece together, only a puzzle made up of different pieces, different places and different people. If it had any meaning, it was for me to figure out, or convince myself I had. I mean, if I *looked* hard enough, or *wanted* it enough, or even just used a little imagination, I guess I'd find one. People usually do. It's like finding faces in things, like rock formations and clouds and toasted-cheese sandwiches. People can find faces in just about anything, given half a chance. Sometimes it's someone very specific, like Jesus or Gandhi or Groucho Marx or someone, but more often it's just some vague idea of a face. What kind of looks like a nose here, maybe a mouth there, a couple of what could possibly pass for eyes over there. I guess we see them because we want to see them, because we need to see them. They already exist inside our heads. But just because we're preconditioned to find something doesn't mean it's really there.

But that's okay, because even if they are only rocks, or clouds, or toasted-cheese sandwiches, or whatever, big deal. I'd rather see something for what it was than see it for what I wanted it to be, any goddam day.

'Look!' I said. 'Down there. That's the exact same spot where I stepped off the kerb into the path of that speeding car. Boy, it seems like a lifetime ago. Longer. Hey, how long ago was it, anyway?' I couldn't even remember. Sunday couldn't either. Imagine both of us forgetting a thing like that.

There were no speeding cars now. Their drivers and passengers had all clambered out onto their roofs to escape the rising black sludge, but it was already lapping at their feet. A handful of taxicabs floated down Broadway, their drivers still hustling for fares, plucking customers out of the gloop and then throwing them back again if they couldn't pay.

'And look over there. That's the hospital where they took me for observation. *Look!* You can see all the patients escaping!'

They were leaping off window ledges and balconies, swan-diving from the roof. Others were huddled together on makeshift rafts, constructed of hundreds of inflated surgical gloves, while doctors swam alongside, puncturing them with hypodermic needles. Others were balancing on bedpans.

Pretty soon we were floating past a building I'd known my whole life, although I'd never seen it from this angle. Looking down at it like that, I suddenly felt a bit like Mary Poppins or somebody, or Peter Pan. Peter Pan and Wendy on their way to Neverland.

'And that's my very own hearth and home right down there, looking almost cosy from up here. That's my room on the corner, and that's the drainpipe I must've shimmied down a million times. And that's the window Louie Louie broke with a goddam rock the day he came round to tell me you'd said "Hi." Boy. I wonder if they'll keep a light burning in the window for me?'

As I said it a light actually did spring up, at the open third-storey window of my father's den. Then it caught hold of the curtains, and the room suddenly began to go up in flames. I could even see my father inside, and what appeared to be an albino Indian elephant, although it might just have easily been African. My father had his back to the window, and might or might not have been juggling what looked like burning tenpins. If he was it wouldn't have surprised me a bit. He was always up to something or other up in that damn den.

But then I noticed his pants were on fire too, and I wondered if *he'd* noticed. As we drifted on past, I called out, just in case, 'Hey, Dad, your pants are on fire!' but I don't know whether he heard me or not. As we drifted away, the whole place suddenly went up in flames, hissing and crackling behind our backs. I wasn't too worried, though. I knew he had plenty of other pairs.

'And there's old Moriarty's,' I said, as we floated by Louie Louie's and my old hang-out, boarded up, just like I'd imagined it, and closed for business. It already looked like it'd been derelict for years, but someone had painted 'FREE MORIARTY. LOCK UP HOLMES' right across the front, which gave me a real bang. I'd've bet ten bucks I knew who'd done it too. 'Hey,' I said, suddenly thinking of something, 'I wonder if anyone ever bothered to collect old Sandman, or whether he might still be lying there on the floor with his head all caved in?' I couldn't, but I could almost see it. I could almost see him still lying there, with that dopey, surprised look on his face. Poor guy. He was just the kind of guy who would get overlooked that way. Then I imagined him waking up all of a sudden, still with his head all caved in, but with no memory of what'd happened, and finding himself boarded up inside and wondering where everybody had gone, and maybe even making himself a milkshake to pass the time, or maybe a hamburger if he was hungry. Then I imagined him sitting up at the counter, having his snack, and wondering idly why he had such a terrific headache. 'I wonder what ever became of old Moriarty. Boy, I miss him. I really do. I'd have liked to have sent him a letter or something. You know, just to let him know how much he meant to everyone, and how much we all miss him and his milkshakes. Wherever he is, though, I hope he's getting a little shut-eye. I hope he's not so beat.'

And so we drifted slowly on, leaving the city, choked and drowning and sinking under its sea of sludge, far behind. Impossibly far behind, in fact. Impossible to reach by bus or car or even plane, it was now a city beyond reach, or my reach, anyhow. Soon it wouldn't even exist, might never have existed, except in my head. Or Louie Louie's, or Moriarty's, or Sandman's even.

I told her all this, and more, gave her a sort of potted history of my life and times, like a Reader's Digest *David Copperfield* or something. For someone who'd been too shy to even say 'Hi' I was a regular chatterbox. And while anyone else might have told me to shut the hell up (I certainly would have, if I'd had to listen to me), Sunday just listened and smiled, and even laughed in all the right places.

And then we were at the beach, and after I'd told her about the old lady and the sea monster and the penny arcade, I said, 'And that's where I saw you.' We were drifting over the high, craggy headland, where I'd seen her with my telescopic eyes. 'Standing there, teetering on the edge of the world, staring up at the sky. You were so intent on it that it made me look up as well. I hadn't even noticed it before, I was so busy trying not to think about some other stuff. Boy,' I said, 'it was beautiful.'

She did her best to smile up at me by throwing her head back, but ended up with it lying almost horizontally along her shoulder. 'Funny,' she said, 'that was my exact same thought, too.'

That was when I suddenly got an uncharacteristic urge to get all goddam gushy. And when I say uncharacteristic, I mean it. I'm just about the least gushy person I know. Ask any of the girls I've ever dated, and they'll tell you. Not that I've dated that many. To tell you the truth, I've probably only ever been on half a dozen dates in my entire life. And as a general rule, they didn't go all that well. They did occasionally, but as a general rule they didn't. I think the problem was mostly that I wasn't really mature enough to be dating in the first place. I probably should have stuck with playing sport, as dumb as most sport is. Or reading books, as dumb as most books are. At least until I was fifteen or sixteen, anyway. Before fifteen or sixteen, it's almost impossible to date successfully. After fifteen or sixteen, I suspect, it becomes a lot easier. Everyone suddenly turns into Romeo and Juliet or something. Everyone's suddenly either hanging about on balconies waiting to be addressed in blank verse, or else wandering around *looking* for people hanging about on balconies to address their blank verse *to*. If you ask me, that old Shakespeare has a lot to answer for, with all that goddam blank verse. Of course, he was a fantastic writer and everything, and a lot of his characters, like Hamlet and whoever, had some really terrific lines, but someone really should have told him to put a sock in it. Anyway, as I was saying, although I'm the *least* gushy person I know, I suddenly had an uncharacteristic urge to gush. I wouldn't even have minded being able to speak in old Shakespeare's blank verse for once. What I wanted to do was tell her just how beautiful she was, and how I still got a knot the size of a fist in what was left of my guts just thinking about her, and how if she could only hold her crazy, wobbling head still long enough, I'd really, really, *really* like to plant one right on her. But then, just when I'd made up my mind to do it, but before I had the chance, there was a terrifically loud *BANG!* and I felt the air suddenly being sucked right out of our balloon.

I looked down and there on the ground was the crazy clown from my dreams, the one who'd given Louie Louie the balloon to give to me. He was holding a smoking blunderbuss under one arm and waving us in like a flight controller with the other. He certainly had gorgeous timing, that's for sure.

50

We fell at a surprisingly stately pace, still hanging from
the shreds and tatters of the burst balloon. Strangely
enough, I guess because of the stately pace of our descent
and everything, we weren't the least bit alarmed at having
been suddenly potshotted out of the sky by a smiling
clown (smiling, not grinning – I was glad to see he'd
cheered the hell up). In fact, quite the opposite. I thought
it might be a good opportunity to say what it was I'd
wanted to say after all, about how beautiful I thought
she was and everything, but once again I never got the
chance. The reason I didn't this time was because before
I'd even had time to open my mouth, I noticed something
I hadn't noticed before: dimples. I can't tell you how
much I like dimples. I don't know how I hadn't noticed
a thing like that before, but I hadn't. And then I thought
that there were probably a thousand and one other little
things about her that I hadn't noticed as well, that I'd
like to have noticed. It'd probably take years and years
to notice them all. And that made me think about all
the things I wanted to say to her, and how that'd probably take years and years as well, so what I did then
was I just kissed her instead. I propped up her lolling
old broken-necked head, and I just planted one right on
her lips.

51

I don't know how long we kissed for, but the next thing I knew the ground was quite a bit closer. We seemed to be coming down in the middle of a picture postcard of rolling green countryside, the afternoon sun glinting off a distant church spire, so corny and beautiful it could break your heart. I could even hear the sound of the church bells pealing gently on the breeze, and I wondered who might have been pealing them, if that's the right word, but not who they might've been pealing for. I knew that much. It was all so corny and beautiful that I didn't know whether to laugh or cry, or neither, or both. Then there was suddenly thick, lush grass right beneath us, and I noticed that, cut into it, there was a freshly dug hole, the perfect size for two. Its steep, straight sides and soft bed of earth looked cool and inviting, and standing around it was a small gathering of people, looking up and waving at us with smiling, shining faces.

Everyone was there. The crazy old lady from the beach, with her pram full of dolls, and Sandman, with the back of his head still all bashed in (so he wasn't still roaming round inside Moriarty's after all). The Viking from across the street and the two talkative ambulance guys who still looked like they thought I'd landed on my head. The doctor who'd been so fond of my unintentional joke (he tipped me a friendly wink), the driver of the car I'd stepped in front of and the midget cop with the well-fitting uniform. Even the three big-headed freaks (so there were three of them at least), each still clutching its crazy box, all knobs and wires, and the somersaulting monkey looked pleased to see us.

And of course Mother was there too, as inappropriately dressed as ever, wearing this long, flowing, terrifically elegant evening gown with a very plunging neckline. I have to admit she looked good. I could almost see what everybody saw in her, or used to, once upon a time when she'd been such a famous beauty and everything. And standing right beside her was good old Louie Louie, who was busy jiggling imaginary breasts and grinning his head off.

Then they all started to applaud as we gently descended, coming to rest at the bottom of the welcoming hole. It felt every bit as cool and inviting as it had looked, the bed of freshly turned earth soft and spongy to the touch.

'What kept you?' Louie Louie asked, instead of jiggling imaginary breasts now giving my mother's ass a proprietorial pat.

'Hey, Louie Louie,' I told him, 'get your hand off my mother's ass, why don'tcha!'

But my mother, happy and beaming like a schoolgirl in love, just said, 'It's all right, dear. Congratulate us. We're married!'

I stared at them both. *'Married?'* I said. 'But what about Dad?'

'Oh, haven't you heard? He's run off with the circus. Apparently that's what he's been doing in his den all these years. Practising his juggling.'

'But I've only just seen him,' I told her. 'His pants were on fire.'

My mother laughed. 'All part of the act, apparently. There's something to do with an elephant too, I believe.'

Louie Louie looked exactly like the cat that'd swallowed the canary. Or is it something to do with a saucer of cream? Anyway, that's what he looked like, if you can imagine it.

'So,' he said, still licking his whiskers and almost purring with satisfaction. He'd ditched the Uzi by now. I don't know what he'd done with it. 'I guess that makes me your new dad.' He paused just long enough to let it sink in, then he gave the knife a good hard twist. '*Son.*'

I know it might seem like a fate worse than death, having old Louie Louie as a stepdad, but you can learn to live with just about most things, I guess, even that.

'Hey, Louie Louie,' I said.

'Call me Dad,' he said.

'Hey, Dad,' I said, just for the hell of it, which really cracked old Louie Louie up. 'Whatever happened to old Moriarty?'

He'd been on my mind quite a lot, and when I'd seen everybody there, waiting for us like that, I'd expected to see him as well. Before Louie Louie could reply, though, I heard it. A goddam dump truck rumbling towards us. It reversed right up to the lip of the hole and then stopped. Old Moriarty himself stuck his head out the window and I was pleased to see he didn't look nearly so beat. Wherever he'd been, he'd obviously been getting some sleep. He looked twenty years younger, almost. He gave me a friendly salute and I gave him one back.

'Hey, Louie Louie,' I said again. 'Do you want to know something?'

'You're a retard and I'm not.'

'Ha, goddam ha. Actually,' I said, 'I think this is the end.'

Louie Louie smiled, and there was actually a tear in his eye. I was going to miss that sonuvabitch.

'I think you're goddam right.'

Moriarty crunched a lever, and the back of the dump truck began to rise. As we lay there at the bottom of the hole, gazing up at a perfect blue square of sky, hard and bright and brittle as glass, we heard its load begin to shift.

'Hey, you know what?' I asked.

'What?' said Sunday, squeezing my hand.

'It was always going to have a happy ending,' I said.

www.vintage-books.co.uk